SEASON OF THE MONSTER

PART II | SUMMER

AJ HUMPHREYS

Season of The Monster | SUMMER was originally produced serially through Amazon's Kindle Vella.

Amazon Kindle Vella Edition / ASIN B0B4P9B3Q2 / June - October 2022

Print First Edition / ISBN 979-8-9867050-2-6 / February 2023

E-Pub First Edition / ISBN 979-8-9867050-3-3 / February 2023

Cover Design: AJ Humphreys

Cover Images: Canva Pro Stock Photos

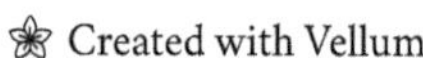 Created with Vellum

PRAISE FOR THE "SEASON OF THE MONSTER" SAGA

"SUPERBLY WELL-WRITTEN WITH PITCH-PERFECT PACING"

"Buckle up for thrills, chills, and plenty of spine-tingling action and suspense in this high octane thriller/suspense novel. Riveting!"

— KRISTINE L. | REEDSY DISCOVERY

"A RARE TREAT"

"It has been a long time since I've taken the time to read a story in completion so fast but I was drawn to the monsters, trying to figure out what they were and if Ghini ever gets her daughter back."

— C.J. LANDRY

"WELL-PACED, UNSETTLING, & LEFT ME CRAVING FOR MORE!"

"The writing style is easy to get into, and the story like-wise. It sucks you into this world which doesn't seem that far off from reality."

— ESMÉE L.

For Everyone Battling Those Monsters Of The Mind.
Never Forget.
You Were Strong Enough To Create Them.
You Are Strong Enough To Defeat Them.

CONTENTS

Preface   ix
PART II | SUMMER   xvii

1. First Light   1
2. Visions   8
3. Duplicity   13
4. Vespids   16
5. Maternal   24
6. Itch and Scratch   30
7. Rise And Shine   37
8. Momma   47
9. Chiye   53
10. Heroes?   64
11. Eavesdropping   71
12. Pause   78
13. The Black Hills Giant   83
14. Subjects   93
15. Schemes   98
16. The Watering Hole   104
17. Changing   111
18. Surveillance   115
19. Help   119
20. Orders   124
21. Reunited   130
22. Luck   136
23. The Notebook   142
24. Pheromones   151
Acknowledgments   161
Sneak Peak of Part III   163
Chill   164

About the Author   171

PREFACE

Hey there reader!

This is probably weird having the fourth wall broken for you, but this preface *was* written as a recap for Part I of *Season of The Monster | SPRING* when *SUMMER* had originally been published serially on Amazon's Kindle Vella.

If you're a fan of a good old-fashioned highlight recap before diving back into your favorite TV show's new season, then what follows is for you.

Not for you?

Skip the preface.

You've been warned.

So, sit back, relax, and enjoy the recap!

P.s. Seriously. If you want to dive straight in, skip the preface and go straight to Chapter 1, you won't be missing anything new. I promise.

Six months had passed since the disappearance of Jeannie Freeman captivated the citizens in and around the Black Hills of South Dakota. Since then, her mother, Ghini, has sacrificed much of her life to keep the search efforts going. Once a reality TV star, she has depleted most of her life's savings trying to dig up anything she can to bring her thirteen-year-old daughter home.

She has few friends. At best there's Todd Dexter — her platonic work bestie — and Samuel Clemens — her father figure and moral support. After that, she has Detective Dakota Johnson and his counterpart Jontay Legends that she can count on. And there are not many more after that.

Dakota, or "Dak," as friends call him, has never given up hope of finding Jeannie. His tenacity spurs an investigation that comes to a head after the discovery of CCTV footage documenting a strange woman. A woman who's the spitting image of a young Ghini. Not only that, she looks to be wearing the tattered and dirty remnants of Jeannie's pajamas. The ones she'd last been sighted wearing.

> "I don't know. I'm an old dog Ghini. Been doing this a long time, and seen a lotta things that I'd never want nobody to see. But this." Dak pauses. The final commitment to what he'll say next. "This hurts my head. Cuz my gut . . . See, it's hollering that that's Jeannie. But how's she go and grow up a decade in six months?"

Meanwhile, a mysterious woman named Queenie has begun assembling a colony of women that she refers to as *her daughters,* hidden within the forests of the Black Hills. Hypnotizing and assimilating each new captive with the use of their '*hive eyes*' and a '*Queen's kiss*' — filled with an intoxicatingly sweet nectar-like saliva — she has steadily grown their ranks.

> She recalls visions of men wrapping her in a coffin, like the mummies at the museum. A see-through prison where she watched the queen leave, while her men stayed behind to protect the tomb. She was finally coming to accept that none of this was a dream, even if it still feels like one. She can hardly bring herself to accept that this is her body. She looks like her mother does on those old VHS tapes that she's not supposed to watch. *Save for the eyes.*

Things begin to change for the colony when Mel comes along. A daughter who seems to be branching off on her own, testing the limits of her abilities, which consistently appear well above average in comparison to those of her sisters'. It appears she was able to do almost anything that Queenie could, including assimilating women *and* men with her own nectary saliva.

All the while, her sister, Kari — Queenie's 'first born' — has been wary of the girl. From the day the girl had hatched, she had noticed something off about her.

In the early days, Kari had felt as if she had been *rescued* by Queenie. She still does. Her mother saved Kari from the avarice of a detestable boyfriend, and the monotony of her own life. But it had just been the two of them in the beginning.

There were more and more daughters of Queenie hatching each day. More responsibility, more time *not* spent with Queenie one on one . . . and now there was Mel, who had also caught their mother's eye. That sibling rivalry eventually bore jealous violence from Kari unto her sister.

Despite the aggression, Mel never seems fazed. She has

other concerns. So she explores, experimenting with the powers she now possesses. Seeing fit, she also adopted a new name. "Velvet." After shaving her head, her fuzzy red hair reminded an insect-enthusiast sister of hers, named Sierra, of a Velvet Ant.

> "That name. It suits my new life. I feel — I feel like this was who I was meant to be. My *perfect* version."

As the warm weather of Spring has swept through the area, Ghini has taken to investigating this mystery with a little help from her friend, Samuel Clemens. Clemens — no relation to the author — has been a staple of the Black Hills community for decades and was there for Ghini in the early days of Jeannie's disappearance.

And as it just so happens, Samuel has a family member who might be able to shed light on this woman with the mysterious eyes.

After arriving in the tiny town of Interior, South Dakota, the pair meet with Samuel's nephew Bernie, who happens to be a trans-man.

When Bernie (at the time Bernice) was twelve, she'd been assaulted and kidnapped by a woman with peculiar eyes and disturbing questions.

> "Know how if you look at someone's eye just right you see the pupil is just like a hole, and the colored part is all these noodles or threads or ripples or whatever? Yeah, well her eye was like a honeycomb of that. Not a drop of white. The noodles wormed their way throughout her entire eye. So, it was full of these brownish-amber threads. And instead of one pit, she's got this collection of oval-ey stopsign holes through-

out. I don't even know how to explain it right. Next thing I know, I come-to in a cave. Her eyes, then cave."

Ghini struggles to reconcile this information with the reality she knows. Something that unfortunately frustrates the quiet and reserved Samuel to the point that the pair end their trip with a dense animosity between them.

So, Ghini goes out on her own to do more research at the one place anyone can find info freely, the public library. But someone has been watching her, and they make their move when she gets up for a coffee. The unknown watcher leaves a note on the keyboard.

You're looking in the wrong place.

Along with the message, is a phone number. But on her [computer] screen is a close-up of an insect's eye. She reads the caption:

`Pseudopupils are common to many families`
`of insects including moths, butterflies,`
`and several species of wasps.`

She inevitably calls the number that evening after getting off work. It's difficult, but she soon gets the woman to trust her enough to begin opening up, only for Ghini's phone to die.

It is several days later when the number finally calls her back at three in the morning. Though the caller sounds different than before.

The woman on the other end identifies herself as K, and speaks as if she is an expert on not only insects but monsters and lore as well. She explains to Ghini how these creatures may have come to be. But then, after a long monologue, K begins acting strange. Abruptly, she abandons the call altogether. Leaving Ghini with many unanswered questions.

During this time, Velvet begins growing a second colony in seclusion, away from the rest of her sisters except for one — Sierra. The girl had been hypnotized and manipulated into coming to the colony by Kari, but assimilated at first by Velvet. Sierra quickly became Velvet's right hand and helps her bolster this surreptitious hive.

That is until Sierra's wealthy parents arrive from Texas, in search of their lost daughter. The extended search efforts led Detectives Johnson and Legends to a piece of evidence that could help track down Sierra's whereabouts.

Unfortunately, what they find only alerts them to a new mystery. There are indications that suggest four men have disappeared from a camping trip in The Black Hills, and they may have had a run-in with Queenie.

When Detective Legends goes back to the crime scene with a pair of uniformed officers, he is stunned and concerned with how quickly one of them, Officer Willow Bradley, locates Sierra.

Out of nowhere, Velvet appears, while Sierra continues to taunt and distract him. Officer Bradley's hand is then revealed, as she had already been assimilated into the hive. It is then that the women capture and assimilate Legends into their ancillary colony.

As *SPRING* came to an end, we learned that Samuel may have one more trick up his sleeve. A contact on a Native American reservation, capable of shedding more light on the situation. Thankfully, Ghini has done her part to patch things up, and together, they have made plans to go pay this contact a visit.

Meanwhile, we learn that K was, in fact, Sierra all along. And now the mysteries of the truth are more clouded than ever.

In the prime hive, Queenie and Kari continue to grow their colony. Both women remain wary of Velvet because they know she is an *alpha*. As Queenie explained to Kari, this is essentially one of their own capable of becoming a queen, should they perform some unspoken ritual.

Then there is Dak. The detective has noticed a change in his old protégé Legends, his behavior seems off. But his larger concerns are a vague awareness of a group of potentially violent women in the forest. Only, he doesn't have the first idea as to what dangers truly lurk within the wilds of the Black Hills.

Now, it's Dak who may be beginning to draw paranormal conclusions. But he fears most for Ghini, whom he had previously shared a relationship with long before these events.

There you have it.

Hopefully, a decent recap of *SPRING*. New readers, I highly recommend going back and reading *SPRING* as a prequel, if you enjoy *SUMMER*. To read that story in its entirety, check out the QR code on this book's back cover.

Here's to SUMMER!

Cheers.

AJ

PART II | SUMMER

1

FIRST LIGHT

Todd is grateful for this warm morning air. He knows summer heat and humidity are right around the corner, but ever since he and Maria began dating, life has been, well, *magical.* This morning is one of the most yet.

The sun has barely poked its first rays over the eastern Badlands. The sky glows with a bounty of colors as he and Maria enjoy their morning stroll alongside her little Yorkie, Kelso. He's a goofball of a dog, but Todd is as much infatuated with Kelso as he is Maria.

This particular morning they're walking around the House of Japan Gardens. A quaint little area with cherry-blossom trees, a veiny spiderweb of footpaths, and four miniature ponds that geese love to frequent. The main features are the old-fashioned, arcing, red, Japanese garden bridges that cross the ponds, leading to grass mounds perfect for a picnic — when not covered in goose excrement.

As they stroll through the vein-like walkways, the pair take a fork on one of the paths. Kelso, ever the curious pup, goes to sniff the bush in the center of the intersecting stony paths. Maria gives him a quick tug, pulling up on his harness, calling for a 'heel.' Only, the little goober remains persistent. His attempts become increasingly more desperate as he tries to get his sniffer into that bush. Thankfully, it seems that a training treat from Maria's fanny pack is motivation enough to distract Kelso and bring him back to her side. However, not without engaging in one last stare-down against that pesky bush.

Todd looks back wondering what the little guy smells. Maybe some birds or squirrels have taken up refuge in there. Though it's more likely some lazy asshole just shoved their garbage between the branches. Or another dog marked it, or —

Wait what was that?

"Did you hear that?" Maria had heard it too.

It sounds silly to Todd, but he could have sworn he heard — *giggling.*

"I don't know. Maybe?" He looks down into her big caramel eyes. "It kinda sounded like . . ." He looks back to the bush as the path bends around one of the ponds. "Ah, never mind. I think it's just a bit early and we're hearing things."

"Oh, my big baby. Are you spooked handsome?" Maria laughs and playfully nudges him with her arm.

He knows they have to be a funny sight. She's all of 5'1" in her running shoes, while Todd stands nearly seven feet tall. But she's been good for him. It hasn't been a long *official* relationship, but it's been the best he's ever had. Their ritual involves walking Kelso early in the mornings, which has been helping his knees and hips more throughout the day. They still ache, but nowhere near as bad. He feels loose and has managed to even drop a few pounds.

"As long as I have you, I can never be spooked, my beautiful Latin goddess." He leans down and offers his lady a kiss, which she takes with a fervor that lets him know what will be in store when they get back to her house.

"Where have you been all my life Todd Dexter?"

"Right here. I'm kinda hard to miss!" It's one of those moments of shared laughter that seems to sync the entirety of the couple's worlds.

Now hand in hand, they follow Kelso's lead as he tugs against his harness to take the bridge over one of the ponds. It's a bit darker here, as a large grove of blossoming trees blots out a patchwork of the morning's rays.

A fluttering sound catches Todd's attention. It looks like Kelso may have heard it too because they both turn and look around them in a state of confusion. All Todd sees are the groves of cherry blossoms and large drooping willows.

As they continue their venture, Todd's head remains on a swivel until he hears a shattering cry from the woman beside him. It's a piercing screech that slices through the early morning air. Her legs come out from under her. Thankfully, Todd's reflexes are quick this morning, and he somehow manages to catch her by the armpit before she wipes out entirely. Frozen in mid-descent, he notices the sheer terror carved into her face.

"What happened?"

"I slipped on something." She huffs out through ragged breaths.

Todd looks around and can sort of make out something on the bridge a step behind them. It's a pile, but the shadows and early morning hues make it hard to discern anything beyond an amorphous blob. Todd's first thought is goose droppings, but the ambiguous mass is too large and curiosity eats at his fingertips, which slide into his pocket and grasp his aging cell phone. He flips out the antiquated device and turns on the flashlight to get a better look.

Instantly, Maria gasps loud enough that a group of robbins decide to flutter skyward at the minor disturbance. She rips Kelso back to her side, keeping him close. "Dios Mio! Is that what I think it is?"

Todd crouches his giant frame down to get a closer look. His knees pop like a firecracker going off. What he finds as he settles on his heels, is a pile of — *meat*. Red meat. It looks too lean to be from the usual suspects, but maybe someone dropped their groceries, and its shape has just morphed while sitting out overnight.

He can see where Maria's heel caught the edge of the pile and she slid forward. The slick trail had to have been close to a foot in length. No wonder she was startled.

"Todd, I don't like this. I think I just heard someone — *giggling.*"

Todd nearly leaps off his feet at that word — *giggling.*

With a cautious strength, he rests his hand on the small of her back. He wants her to know he is here for her.

"Listen, if you're out there, this ain't funny!" He looks back to Maria and takes her hand in his. "Let's get movin', we got a long day ahead, anyway."

She smiles up at him. She is quite possibly the most emotionally strong person he knows, behind Ghini of course. But, even though Maria does well to hide her fear, Todd can see the panic pressing against her soft round features. He'll be the strong one. Getting them back home without issue is his main priority right now. He knows it's all probably nothing, but quickly takes a photo of the meat pile, feeling that if it isn't *nothing,* and therefore is *something,* he will need to prove it to someone.

As he steps off the bridge, he knows he's heard that

giggling again. Maria must have too because she looks up at him. Deep, doe-like eyes widen with a clear expression of worry and fear. He keeps a tight hold on her hand, and she returns the favor. He cannot help but appreciate how strong the tiny woman's grip is.

Suddenly, there's that fluttering sound again. It's subtle and quiet, but unmistakable. They increase their pace, and Todd does his best to not let his strides get too long. But Maria's no slouch and hurries her short, powerful legs with a fervor that seems all too common of women who share her stature.

WOOOF! WOOOF! WOOOF!

Kelso's barks shatter the heart-pounding silence before quickly turning to a guttural growl. The sun peaks over the hills, showering the little pathway in a sea of warm golden glow. Just then, two young women, more like girls, materialize from the shadows. Despite thinking how young the pair are, Todd's first observation is that they are significantly over-dressed, wearing thermals, vests, and stocking caps on this warm summer morning.

Kelso continues to bark and growl. His ears pin straight back against his skull as his lips inch backward into a snarl. Maria holds his leash tightly, fighting off the dog's continued desire to press low and forward toward the two girls.

One of them, young and dark-skinned steps forward, "Good morning. How's it going?" She has an unsettling sneer on her face.

Todd places himself between the girls and Maria, who has managed to wrangle Kelso to her side. Todd is not sure what *this* is, but the situation feels wrong. Like one false move could mean life or death. It's a sense he's honed throughout his lifetime. "We just walking. What you and yours doin'?" His nerves confound his mind into shortened bursts of words.

Maria screams before Todd realizes anything has

happened. Slowly, his mind registers a tight burning pinch in his thigh. Something hot eats away at his nerves as if he'd just poured rubbing alcohol or *IcyHot* all over a series of deep cuts. That's when he looks down, finally noticing that the other girl is right there in front of him.

In his space.

Dark curly black hair hangs just above her shoulders. She looks familiar, but he can't place her. Where would he know a little white girl from? Maybe one of the boys' basketball games?

"Hi there. I'm Sierra. And, you and I, we're gonna be friends."

Todd looks down past the girl's unsettling grin to see her pale fingers end at his shorts. No, not end. Her fingernails are completely buried into the meat of his thigh. There's an unsettling fluid pumping beneath the surface of her fingers. It's like something out of a nightmare. Whatever the liquid is, looks to be flowing toward the fingernails concealed within his quad. He can feel it pulsing and burning as it enters his bloodstream, like a hot injection.

This can't be real!

The last things he sees before blacking out, are Kelso high-tailing it out of the park with the leash flapping behind him, and the other girl — the little sister with the sneer on her face — standing over Maria, whose luxurious cocoa-colored hair lies in the grotesque meat pile, while her caramel eyes seem to drain of their natural luster.

He only thinks about what could've been. This woman whom he'd thought was helping him find happiness. A life he could tell his best friend, Ghini, about. He'd had images of one day going on double dates with Ghini and some new man in her life, all the while Maria and he would let little Jeannie babysit...

Instead, there is the reality of the moment. Maria's hand limply rests across her throat. A deep dark scarlet courses between her fingers, while a faint and final gurgling cough worms its way across her lips.

The little sister's hand is held high. As if in slow motion, Todd notes her fingertips, capped with tiny barbs, which drip that same visceral red. Each drop appears to glow as they fall to the Earth below, reflecting a similar color from the silhouetting sky's first dawning lights.

2

VISIONS

"I don't like this idea, Queenie." Kari avoids Mel's vicious glare, continuing as if her sister weren't there. "I think beginning to build up a stockpile of drones is necessary and all, but this plan sounds . . . *reckless*. Why would we sacrifice our clandestine isolation for this gambit?"

Mel leans silently against the wall, her lips pursed, not saying a word. Though, she is loving the sight of Kari working herself up, throwing out five-dollar words in a desperate attempt to win their mother over.

"Oh sweet, caring, Kari. Always by my side, just like I'd hoped. But your sister makes a valid point. Though, it seems you may not have been listening *closely*."

Kari's bold cheekbones flush with embarrassment at the clear insinuation of her selfish and willful ignorance. "Queenie, I swear! I've *been* listening! But, you said it yourself, she's a —"

Queenie's eyes flash a near-neon glare that freezes the next words to her tongue. Kari knows she is done speaking. A fear envelops her as the thought of the slightest peep elicits a deep dread that looms with sinister malice. Kari can't name a time specifically, or even a rational explanation as to why, but for some untold reason, she gets the sense that her mother has been irritable as of late and her anger might result in the eruption of furious geysers.

Images within her memory that don't feel real begin slithering through her. A sister. *Kitty*. That's what they'd called her. She was dead now.

But how? Why?

Maybe it had just been a vivid dream. Had she made the girl up?

No.

She doesn't dream anymore. None of them do.

But there's something else there. Something more important.

Where was the body?

But why is that the question?

Images of Queenie's face flash through her mind. Those neon eyes. Eyebrows arched violently in anger. A silence so loud it became deafening. None of it makes sense and for a moment Kari fears she might faint right there in front of her mother and sister.

A small clip plays out inside her memory. The woman's — *Kitty's* — body collides head-first with a wall before falling limp like a rag doll. The memory zooms through her with disorienting speed.

"May I, Mother?" A tone of arrogance burns in Kari's ears. She forces herself back to reality, her eyes drawn to the nuisance of a sister. But somehow, despite feeling more lucid, she finds her feet still frozen by fear, and maybe something *more*.

Queenie gives a curt nod that Kari craves, knowing it isn't intended for her.

"See Kari, here's the thing. All Sierra has to do is return to her parents before they leave town, which they will. But that doesn't mean they'll stop looking for her. So, if instead, we have Willow *find* a lead," she makes a display of air quotes around the word, "and share it with that detective. Well, then the pair can *track down*," again with the air quotes, "Sierra, who will have unfortunately been the victim of a kidnapping. Then once Sierra brings her parents back here, we can turn Mom and Dad, and the three of them will be able to throw the scent off the disappearances. Not to mention, the fortune that Queenie will then have at her disposal. There'd be no need to live in a cave anymore, we could covertly buy whatever we wanted."

The flash of a nod lets Kari know that Queenie is okay with her speaking once more. The apprehensive fear abates, but still, she feels the dregs of her haunting imagination creating those terrifying images lying in wait.

There's Kitty on the ground. Her neck bent at an impossible angle. Her eyes were so normal, so empty. But then she's gone and Kari's confused.

She needs to stay focused.

Her mother wants her to speak. But, there isn't any fight or fury in Kari now. Not with her mind feeling so jumbled. An image of Queenie, her back turned to Kari, flashes and she avoids the train of thought. Time stretches on, and she is silent despite her mother's unspoken request for her input.

"Okay sure, I mean, that sounds great and all. But what if something goes wrong, and they figure out that we exist? The police I mean. We don't want to draw attention to ourselves! We will, out in the open!" Kari is almost whining. She hears it too, but she feels strongly and passionate about this. Yet, her eyes keep darting back to Queenie, aware of the boiling anger that she senses emanating from her mother.

"Kari, we wouldn't even be dealing with this issue if you hadn't gone so far as to pull the girl from a nightclub in the first place!" Mel chides. The look on her face is confident and snide. "But you did it, and now *we* are dealing with it."

"Do you understand sweet Kari?" Queenie's eyes shine like polished amber. The thought is communicated behind them.

If you can't comprehend, I will be required to force your understanding.

The fight leaves Kari's chest. Her shoulders slump as she relents to the hefty weight of her mother's gaze. "Okay. Just tell me what you need from me." She can't help but stare at the floor.

Those bright eyes haunt her with fragments of memories. Bloody lips. Kitty's body flying through the air. Then it lay broken on the cave floor. Then it's gone. Her head hurts with the confusion of these reveries.

Looking up, she meets the ferocious stare of Mel's blue whirlpools. She knows the bitch wants nothing more than a fight. Kari can still remember their first altercation. She'd thrown the little nuisance into the wall. She'd slammed her like a hockey goon, but Queenie had stopped her.

Then it's the images of Kitty again.

Someone had thrown her. Faster. And harder than Kari ever could.

An image of lush, dark, blood-stained lips flashes through her mind, and Kari once more thinks she might faint.

"Then it is settled. Mel, get together with Willow and Sierra. Finalize the plan by tonight. Then execute it."

Mel gives a quick nod and flips her eyes back to normal, as she makes a brisk exit from the chamber where the three of them have held their little counsel of minds this morning.

"As for you sweet Kari, *come here* my firstborn." Her mother stretches out long arms that encircle Kari in a tight yet tender embrace as soon as her legs seem to maneuver her close enough. "Oh, Sweet Kari, please know that jealousy is not a good color on you."

The honeyed scent of Queenie's natural odor eases Kari's anxiety. It reminds her that the greatest woman she's ever known is here. Right before her. She looks into the glowing, pulsing amber honeycombs of her mother, and she is reminded that Queenie will always be here to take care of her. Nothing eases those stressful memories for Kari more than that comforting knowledge.

3

DUPLICITY

When Velvet arrives at *The Mud Hole,* which happens to be the stupidest name in the world — one Velvet can't believe stuck — she finds Sierra and Dezi talking with Willow.

"Where are all the others?"

The trio turns to look at her with excitement on their faces. "It's already worked." Dezi pipes up. Excitable as ever, the girl always seems to infect the room with energy.

"Great news. But there's greater news on my part." Velvet says pulsing her eyes in the girls' direction. "Queenie has given the all-clear. So, it's time to sacrifice our sweet innocent Sierra and her parents. But this was inevitable, no?"

Sierra lets out her now-infamous snort, and Velvet takes note that the girl has done well to re-don her emo-girl aesthetic. "Everything's set up and ready. Though I will say, I'm going to miss our little *mud hole.*" She snickers, not quite giving in to her full-blown nasally chortle.

"It has been good to us, hasn't it?" The three women nod in unison with Velvet's words, recalling how much they'd accomplished down in this little pit. "Well then *Willow*, get on back to work, Queenie will want to make sure you're there. You know she has an interest in Legends and the other detective. The old fat one. So, let's make sure that you're in place if she has any other pigs in the barn. Sierra, you're coming back with me tonight, and what do we tell Queenie the plan is?"

In a monotone voice with her eyes nearly rolling out of her head, she imitates the caricature of herself. "Like, we made sure to make it look like I've been locked in a dungeon or whatever. Then it's like, I'm totally going to be found after escaping some creep's cellar. I'll totally be like, uh, yeah I escaped after he tried to ya know have his way with me."

Velvet's eyes flip and pulse an icy fury that reminds Sierra who is in charge here, and what will happen if she doesn't take things seriously.

The girl begins an impressive display of acting as tears flow down from her eyes. "Thankfully, I managed to escape! Thank the Almighty above for Officers Bradley and Legends. They were like my knights in shining armor." She heaves through crocodile tears that must have been learned from her mother. "They like totally saved my life." She gasps, feigning a solitary moment of collection. "Mommy, Daddy, I was so uh-scared." She lets the waterworks flow unbridled now.

"Good." Velvet turns her attention to Willow. "Officer Bradley. Your role?"

"I receive an anonymous tip about screams, to which Detective Legends will take the lead and require my assistance. Upon a thorough canvassing of the area, we will locate Ms. Kalisch. After which, Detective Legends and I will proceed to notify the girl's parents who will have returned to their hotel in time for us to *reunite* the family."

Velvet swells with pride. Lastly, she turns to Dezi. Her happy-go-lucky daughter reminds Velvet of Letitia Wright in

Black Panther. "Don't worry about me Moms! I've got my ish done!" She laughs quickly but manages to don a serious face in a flicker. "All the girls are where they are supposed to be. Three at each spot. Your new wig is in the alcove, and the uniform is pressed and clean. Are you sure you want to do this though?" The look on her face is one of genuine concern. But, Velvet isn't phased. "Okay. But if you change your mind, Marta is easily capable of doing exactly what she's told. The lady isn't bright Moms."

They all laugh. The woman isn't bright but she was a genius acquisition by Dezi and Sierra. Thanks to their quick thinking, they now had everything they'd needed to get into the hotel where the Kalisch's were staying.

"Then we have it. The Kalisch's will be up bright and early tomorrow morning. Dezi, you'll be with Marta, and make sure that the pair are to their rooms no later than nine A.M."

"Roger that Moms!" She salutes.

Velvet doesn't bother to acknowledge the girl's theatrical response this time. "Now Sierra, it's time that you look the part for tomorrow. *This won't hurt a bit.*" She watches as the girl's face goes slack. She looks like a porcelain doll with her hefty makeup and ivory skin. "Todd." She whistles as she would for a dog, and the large man heaves himself from the shadows with a flat gaze that says he will do anything that Velvet tells him.

"Make it look like our little Sierra has been the victim of an episode of SVU."

The giant nods before slamming his gargantuan fist into the girl's eye. Though she hardly flinches, Velvet is anxious about the results. She hopes the big man can leave plenty of bruises and wounds.

4

VESPIDS

"Uggghhhhh this is unbelievable!" Ghini groans while slumping further into the passenger seat of Samuel's F250.

He grunts an affirmative acknowledgment of frustration.

The pair have been on the road since just after five this morning, and their five-hour drive looks as if it will end up being at least a ten-hour trudge thanks to a plethora of highway construction and accidents.

The first incident had been within the city limits and despite the early hour and limited traffic, they'd easily added an hour as the result of a particularly brutal wreck in a construction zone.

The second accident had been easier to navigate. Then came the third incident around the midpoint of their trip. Three cars were totaled in the ditch segmenting the east- and west-bound highways. It felt like the start of a Zombie movie. Considering their current reality, Ghini half expected that this was a sign for the beginning of the end — marking their descent into a living Hell.

They should have been within an hour of the reservation, instead, they pulled off in a tiny town called Murdo. Needing a break from the relentless slowdowns, they took this opportunity to enjoy a quiet meal where neither of them said much. Samuel had coffee and bacon. Ghini a bison burger so thick, it had put her to sleep once they'd gotten back on the road.

When she awoke, they were no longer on the highway. While unconscious, Samuel had transitioned to country roads that should have been desolate but were growing congested with the slew of cars detoured from the interstate.

Now it's mid-afternoon, and even though they are rejoining the flow of highway traffic, everything is moving slowly through one-lane construction. That's when they see the sign for their exit — *closed due to construction.* There's plenty of daylight left, but Ghini feels certain they won't be heading back to Rapid City this evening.

When they finally make their way past the string of flashing lights and orange-vested, sweat-stained DOT workers littering the prairie lands, they find the detour sign instructing them to take the next exit and traverse backward. It feels like a minor miracle once they inevitably whizz past the faded sign reading *Flandreau 10 Mi.*

"Finally! I thought this day was never gonna end." Ghini rubs at the sleep in her eyes. Samuel had told her to expect to arrive around 11:00 am. Instead, the clock now reads 5:02 pm. She could tell that the day has gotten to Samuel as well. The detours, the slowdowns, the extra stops for gas — the price of gas — it all seems to be taking its toll on her grey-haired friend.

"We got a bit further than ten." He says flatly.

She lets that comment sit between them before shooting him a steely glare, *"how much longer . . ."*

This elicits the briefest of snickers from Samuel. Clearly,

the trip has eaten away at his gruff demeanor. "Not much. Need to enter reservation land, not the city."

"And that's . . . how much further . . ."

"Couple-a miles is all."

A sigh escapes Ghini and relief floods her system. Her eyes drift out the passenger window toward fields of corn and beans fluttering past in their hypnotically neat rows. It isn't long before she spots the city on the horizon. Though, calling it a city is probably giving the place too much credit. It's tiny. The battered sign with bullet holes designating the city limits says there are less than two-thousand people living here.

It's an older city. The cracked blacktop streets are predominately littered with aging homes that for the most part, look well-kept and maintained, despite their age. There are some local shops and restaurants, but it appears the place hasn't avoided the onslaught of commercial chain gas stations and restaurants. The illusion of small-town America also feels disrupted by the plethora of billboards advertising for the casino, the church, and the hospital.

"We're crossing into reservation land now," Samuel mutters as they leave the billboards and aging roads behind for more hypnotic lines of endless crops.

Ghini whips her head back and forth looking for a sign. "How do you know? I don't see anything that says that. Shit, I don't see a thing except crops."

Samuel sighs, "Yeah. Not much here but farmland. Few families tend it, but most have taken up in Flandreau-proper. The reservation ain't much anyway. Maybe three n' a-half miles. Few hundred residents at most."

In her mind, Ghini had grand images of what this place would be. A beautiful cultural homage to a people reclaiming their land, but it wasn't much different than all the other rural areas she'd been through. In fact, it is nearly identical, if not worse. Without knowing, it would be impossible to tell whether this was a recognized reservation or some random family's farm, and that saddens Ghini.

"Here we are." Samuel breaks the somber quiet as he turns down a dirt road toward a trio of mobile homes. There are some livestock pens and farming equipment, but other than a few bits of native artwork and carvings, there isn't a thing denoting the inhabitants' cultural roots.

"Kind of disappointing isn't it?" Samuel says as if he's read Ghini's mind.

"Heard that."

The melancholy in the air between them is heavy with the late afternoon humidity as they both disembark from the vehicle.

"Well, it's about damn time Clemens!"

Once more, Ghini is unsure as to what she had expected of their host, but the man in cargo shorts and working denim isn't it. He's got a long braid of hair slung over his shoulder and a neatly trimmed goatee. He's built like a farmer, burly with a beer gut. There's a slight accent, which she recognizes as native, but for the most part, he's fairly nondescript. Maybe that's a good thing, she knows what it means to be a stereotype.

"Manny. Good to see ya." The men share a visibly firm handshake before Manny pulls in Samuel for a hug complete with the loud clasp of back slaps.

Manny laughs while Samuel smirks, and Ghini can't help but think how she's seeing all these sides of Samuel that she'd never known existed. It reminds her that people live lives beyond her worldview. That doesn't change the fact that her current worldview — the one centered on Jeannie — is the only one she cares to let consume her.

"This must be Ms. Freeman. A pleasure ma'am." He says

extending a deep radish-colored hand that grips hers gently despite how it swallows her own amidst a patchwork of rough callouses.

"Nice to meet you too. Manny was it?" He nods gingerly before letting go. "So what do you know about these creatures?" Ghini doesn't want to mince words. It's been a long day and the sun is beginning to color the world with the dark foreboding shades of sundown.

"This one doesn't play around, does she, Clemens!" He slaps Samuel across the back eliciting a gruff stare much more familiar to Ghini.

"We've had a long 'un." He growls toward their host.

"Fair-nuff. Heard bout all the accidents on the news. Think it was a record or something today." He looks to Ghini, and she's certain he can read the look on her face, something akin to, *alright, let's get this show on the road already.* "That's one hell of a glare. 'D-hate to be your man when yer pissed. C'mon then, I guess you want to know why you're here." He checks his watch and looks around before marching off behind the trio of trailers.

In the distance is a fourth mobile home. Manny leads them through a field of crops that reaches up to Ghini's elbows.

A breeze carries the scent of skunk mixed with a piney citrus to Ghini's nostrils. "Is that weed?"

A loud guffaw escapes Manny's gut. "Damn woman! You got a nose on ya! Indeed is. See that field over there," He points toward the east where budding plants grow in the distance. The kind that are without a doubt, neither beans nor corn.

Her nod tells him to go on.

"The reservation is allowed to grow medicinal cannabis. Quite the lucrative business in these parts, but that don't mean it didn't scare off the more conservative members of the tribe." A sigh whispers out from between his lips, "But that's not the only thing that done scared 'em off." The words hang with an ominous air, as the trio navigates their way through the field up to the trailer.

Inside, Manny motions for them to sit down on an old couch straight out of the 80s. The only thing missing is a wallpaper backdrop, but the faux-wood paneling is apt. As they sit, Manny grabs a couple Budweisers from a rusting mini-fridge.

The room is sparse, save for a radio, the couch, the mini-fridge, and several mason jars containing buds of marijuana, neatly organized atop a dull metallic shelf. The room smells of burnt weed. The only thing out of place is a heavy oaken door situated behind the recliner where Manny takes his seat.

A large *BANG* reverberates through the floor without warning. Ghini looks at Samuel, who wears a subtle look of intrigue.

"That's what you done came here to see," Manny says sipping on his beer and rolling a joint with one hand. "Now I owe Samuel all the favors in the world, he's a man that'd never abuse them, and I'm happy to share with him. But why do you want to know miss?"

She catches him up on everything. Jeannie's disappearance, Bernie, Dak's suspicions of women in the Hills, K, and the research from her time spent in the library. Manny appears riveted by the accounts, hardly stirring, except to tuck his now rolled joint behind his ear, before beginning to roll another, which finds a home in the front pocket of his denim.

"Well, I'll be. You definitely are dealing with the Vespids, aren't ya?"

"*Vespids?*"

He nods, "based on Latin for wasps, maybe they shared the name, who knows." He opens another Budweiser and takes a long swig. "I sure don't know about all that stuff this K done told ya, but what I can say with certainty is that these things been around a long time. We used to call them, *wicayazipa*," which sounds like *witch-uh-yahtzee-pah*. "But the white man thought we was talking about *witches*. In a sense they are, but the white man's word's easier for most, so *Vespids* it were."

"Manny." Samuel needn't say more.

"Right. You ain't here for a history lesson. But we got one. We been learning about her. Trying to reverse it. Get her back to normal."

"You have a — *Vespid?*" Ghini startles to her feet.

"Sure do." Another *BANG* beneath the floor shocks Ghini back into her seat.

"That's her." Manny says through a hefty sigh that precedes him striking a match, which scorches the tip of the joint he has removed from behind his ear. "Listen. That woman's family." A sudden rhythmic knock echoes on the strange oak door. With rehearsed movements, Manny gets up and moves the recliner, revealing a slew of deadbolts that he unlocks in succession.

Through the doorway steps another man. He's bald, with a five o'clock shadow, and looks to be a few years younger than Manny. "This is my little brother Lawson."

The younger brother scoffs and smacks Manny on the back before re-engaging the deadbolts. "Neither of us is little, plus you're only older by eleven months. We was born the same year!" He says sharing a laugh with his older brother, which creates a striking family resemblance. Lawson pries the joint away and gives it several puffs before gesturing for Manny to take it back.

"Irish Indian Twins we are!" Manny cackles while assuming responsibility for the burning joint.

Neither Ghini nor Samuel laughs though. The behavior is

unsettling, considering it comes from two people living with a monster underfoot.

"How many people know about her?" Ghini has to know.

The brothers share a prolonged glance at one another before Lawson nods to Manny.

"There're about 600 of us living on the res land, and we all know. But a couple hundred moved to the city. Most took casino jobs cuz they didn't want to be around her, but see —" He looks to his brother with a sadness in his now drooping bloodshot eyes.

"That's our mama down there. She changed when we was nothing more than boys, and we been trying to figure out how to get her back ever since." The forlorn look on his brother's face seems to migrate toward Lawson as he recovers the joint for a long draw. "Most aint comfortable with her. . . She's done things. She escaped once . . . and well, it weren't good. So, we built a special room for her downstairs in the sub-basement."

Manny chimes in. "We'll take ya down there in the morning, she'll be curling up to sleep soon. She sleeps soundly through the night. You'll want to see her when she gets active. We got a guest trailer back by your truck. Y'all can crash there for the night, and we'll pick this up in the mornin'."

A furtive glance passes between Ghini and Samuel before Samuel acknowledges the brothers' offer with a nod.

However, Ghini has one last burning question, "How long has she been down there?"

"Twenty years."

5

MATERNAL

"Oh my. I hardly recognize you, *likkle* one." Queenie says cocking her head to the side. Sierra has returned to her original appearance, bringing a motherly ache of nostalgia to Queenie's chest. Reveries of that first evening with the girl flash through her memory. Except, it looks like Mel has tried to rough the girl up a bit as part of her plan. Albeit, from Queenie's perspective, it's nowhere near enough.

"So, you have finished thinking up a plan I take it?"

Sierra nods, but, of course, it is Mel who steps forward to speak. It seems respectful, but Queenie can't avoid the cynicism ebbing from Kari. Their mother knows the poor girl is incapable of looking past how her siblings might be attempting to manipulate Queenie for their own gain.

"Yes, mother. I think I have just the plan. *Sierra . . .*" The girl turns away from Queenie and peers into the spotted sapphires of Mel's eyes. *"You need to forget this place. You need to listen to every word Queenie and I tell you. You will tell your parents that you ran off —"*

"Pardon the interruption. Queenie, *Velvet* . . ." All eyes pivot to find Lynn standing at the chamber's entrance. There is a near-identical flash of anger on both Queenie and Mel's faces upon the disturbance.

Queenie notes a sense of personal intrigue in exploring the abject disdain Mel now has toward this woman who would have once called herself the girl's *biological* mother. Queenie can recall finding the pair of them out hiking through The Hills like it was yesterday.

It had been Kari's first *'rescue'* — as they had grown to term the process of freeing Queenie's daughters from the horrors of humanity. She recalls that first time she was able to watch a daughter feel the intoxicating burn of the stingers at her fingertips. The way Kari's nails had dripped and the release she'd felt sinking her fingertips deep into Lynn's arm was as much part of Queenie's memories as they were her first-born's. She'd felt her breast swell with pride watching Kari's eyes surge with the pulse of her beautiful honeycombs. She could feel the sense of control that Kari exuded over the women.

Now, Queenie wondered what this experience must be like for Lynn. It's an odd curiosity. Queenie finds the woman quite useless, especially in comparison to her beautiful little redheaded daughter. And now, here was that same daughter, looking down on this maternal figure of hers as if she were nothing more than a parasite. A nuisance. A stain.

"Um, the drones are ready for assimilation." The feeble woman croaks.

A flicker of movement in those dotted sapphires speaks volumes to Queenie. Her own amber hives flicker back the malevolent curiosities of her heart. The conversation is unspoken and speedy. Mel pounces forward with the speed and tenacity of a jungle cat, sending Lynn to the ground with a harsh crash. The woman is frozen beneath the crouched scarlet-haired creature sitting on her chest like a gargoyle.

"You think that's more important than what we're doing right now?" She hisses the spray of words into the wretch's face.

"No."

Queenie can't see either woman's eyes from her tall vantage, but she can picture the pathetic excuse for a daughter's swollen pupils beneath the weight of Mel's bright blues pulsing amidst swelling black holes.

"Then . . ." Mel raises both hands above her head, fingers splayed like claws. The tips are sharp and drip the noxious honey-gold venom that throbs beneath her nails.

"Why . . ."

She swipes her right hand across the woman's face, slicing four deep cavernous trenches through the unsightly fool's brow and cheek.

"Are . . ."

A swipe of her left hand.

"You . . ."

The right again.

"Bothering . . ."

The left once more, followed by both hands screaming back across the entirety of the downed woman's face as Mel screeches out the last word.

"*US?*"

Then, as if nothing happened, she hops off the woman who had birthed her and saunters over to Queenie's side.

Queenie can feel the subtle twitches emanating from sweet Kari nearby. She knows her firstborn desperately wants to aid her mauled sister. Yet, amidst the brutality and weeping slashes, neither Kari nor the assailed woman move an inch. They are both too well trained. They know to wait for their mother's next instructions. Obedient like a well-trained hound.

"There, there my precious Mel. This is your sister after all." Queenie says, placing a motherly arm around the red-headed girl. "Lynn, why don't you go wait with the drones." The words come out as an order, not a question. "I'll be there shortly, okay hon."

"Of course mother." The pathetic presence of the woman as she climbs to her feet, wounds weeping scarlet tears that trace down the entirety of her jawline and neck, sickens Queenie. She is most glad to see the woman removed from her sight.

With the oaf gone, Queenie urges Mel to continue from where they'd been interrupted. "*Sierra.*" The girl nods toward Mel at the mention of her name. "*I need you to tell your parents that you were kidnapped by this here gentleman.*" She points to the incredibly tall black man balled up in the corner of the room.

"*After that, you are to stay with your parents, who will see your true eyes. When they do, bring them to our colony. Then Queenie will assimilate them. Meanwhile, our brother Todd here will tragically lose his life, yet you are to tell them that all of the following things have happened to you while in his clutches.*"

The girl goes on in great detail to describe horrible acts of violence and assault that range from sexual and physical to psychological.

"*Is that understood?*"

Sierra's vacant expression never stirs as she returns a complacent nod. Queenie cannot help but look on with motherly joy, as she once again pulls Mel in for a loving embrace at her side. "Well done my precious Mel. She seems to be adequately under your influence." Queenie plants a kiss atop the girl's fuzzy head, leaving the tiniest, lingering trail of sweet nectar.

However, it's now Queenie's turn. She slowly circles Sierra, while the girl remains frozen in place like a statue. "Now Sierra, is this your only plan?" The girl nods. "No one has asked you to take part in any other tasks or duties?"

"Correct mother."

Queenie need not look to Mel to know that the girl is good. Very good. Kari on the other hand wears a perplexed expression. She's the only one in the room showing any emotion. Otherwise, everyone else in the chamber looks as flat as Sierra.

It's then that Queenie decides to round on Mel, quickly sliding into the girl's space, where she looms over her. Queenie finds joy in watching the little one shudder and shrink those bright blue eyes back to their normal appearance. Her pupils swell wide beneath the weight of her mother's glare. "My precious daughter. Have you given any instructions to Sierra that I do not know about?"

"No mother."

"Interesting." She paces around Mel and takes note of the elation wafting off Kari as she watches this display. "Then you won't mind fetching Ms. Willow for me, would you?"

"It would be my pleasure."

"Go on then."

The streak of red moves swiftly from the chamber, and Queenie finds Kari looking at her with inquiring eyes. But neither says a word. Queenie simply holds a finger to her lips, knowing her firstborn will require no more instruction than that.

When Mel returns, she has Willow in tow behind her.

"Hello mother," the woman says in her deep feminine voice.

"Good evening you wonderful child, you." Once again eyes

give way to Queenie as she begins her interrogation. "What is your plan for tomorrow?"

Methodically she returns the answer, "First, I will arrive promptly to work, where I will locate Detective Legends and inform him that I've been given a tip regarding the whereabouts of the Kalisch girl. I will then ensure that Detective Legends includes me in the bust. We will locate Ms. Kalisch at the home of Todd Dexter. There, Detective Legends and I will not only find and rescue the missing Kalisch girl but discover the body of a missing woman named Maria DeSantos, who unfortunately did not survive. In the heat of the moment, the suspect will discharge a weapon, fortunately missing both Detective Legends and myself. We will then be forced to return fire in self-defense, thus taking the suspect's life."

"Perfect. And after that?"

"I will bring Detective Legends here to you, and ensure that Ms. Kalisch safely re-unites with her parents, who she will then return with for assimilation."

"Excellent. I am so proud of you all." Queenie brandishes large yellowing teeth with a beaming smile. "Lastly, Kari. Sierra must look the part when she's found. I see she already has a few scrapes and bruises, but please give her a black eye and a few more markings, enough to be believable. Just don't go overboard, she is your sister after all."

"Of course mother."

Queenie knows she doesn't need to show her eyes to Kari for this task because her sweet firstborn is all too happy to take out her rage on the girl. Each time her daughter's knuckles connect with the defenseless girl's tender flesh, Queenie can feel the sparks of pride igniting behind her breast all over again.

6

ITCH AND SCRATCH

"Trypophobia."

"Johnson. That's some made-up bull shit."

"*Officer* Paradiso, I said get your fucking phone out of my face." Dak bats the officer's phone away, careful not to knock it out of Paradiso's hand entirely. "I don't know what it's about, or why I'm like this; but shit like *that*, like odd-shaped holes and divots and whatever just makes my skin crawl."

Amidst the overwhelming anxiety coursing through him, his body gives a quick shiver. Knowing he's already visibly flustered, Dak tries to exaggerate the convulsion so it appears to be an act. Only, it's anything but. He catches one last glimpse of the officer's phone before he finally removes it from Dak's sight, and he fears that image will live in his mind rent-free for some time.

It's true. Ever since Dak had been a small child there was something about things like an empty lotus head after it lost all its petals, an open pomegranate, strawberries, honeycombs, and even certain wounds — typically of the hole variety —

that were like nails to a chalkboard for him. And now, he can add moth eyes to that list. Sometimes it's so bad that he has to force himself to get sick to find any sort of relief.

"How the hell are you a cop, man? It's just a bug. And a picture of one, at that. It's not going to hurt you." Officer Paradiso scoffs, turning the screen back on himself. The look on his face is all self-admiration as he becomes re-enamored with the image he'd captured with his swanky new macro-photography camera.

The photo had been so incredibly close-up and *detailed*. The eyes though. Those are what did it. They took up nearly half the screen with their bluish-green hue and several oddly shaped pupils patch-worked throughout. Looking at them felt unnatural. Not the act, but like he'd stumbled upon some sort of — *abomination*. It felt almost alien, and all of those sorts of thoughts were where Dak began to spiral.

If he was being honest with himself, the image instilled a raw fear somewhere deep in his chest.

"I don't know what to tell ya, Paradiso. I don't like that shit. Show it to me again though, and I'll break that damn phone." Dak growls toward the young officer. Paradiso had come to him like a proud child with a crayon drawing for the fridge. The young officer's intention had been crystal clear, hubris. Except, now the uniformed man stalks off like a dog with its tail tucked between its legs.

As his heart, skin, and every neurotic ounce inside of him begins to settle, Dak returns to the email he'd been antici-pating all night. Attached is the report regarding the results of the vocal recognition software that had been utilized to perform an analysis of the two soundbites he'd sent over. The one from the mysterious unsub out in the woods, and the voicemail from Ghini.

> **After a long and thorough examination
> utilizing —**

BLAH - BLAH - BLAH. Dak doesn't care about their scientific method or any of that jazz, he wants the results.

> **Concluding our extensive efforts, my
> team and I feel that we can say with
> ninety-percent certainty that the two
> voices display distinct similarities
> but are not entirely identical. The
> patterns of speech, do however indi-
> cate, with high probability, that the
> two peoples are either related or have
> been cohabitants of the same dwelling
> for an extensive period of time. The
> mannerisms of speech are most similar
> when it comes not only to the inflec-
> tion and intonation of each speaker's
> wording, but the speed and cadence
> employed through each speaker's oration
> tell of a long-standing connection
> between the two individuals. Whether
> that's due to cohabitation with one
> another or a mutual connection, we
> cannot infer further.**

DAK BREATHES out the air he hadn't realized his lungs had been jailing. It's a relief knowing that this isn't Ghini on the video, but at the same time, the improbable machinations of his mind don't seem to be so easily written off as being ridiculous.

There are a plethora of itches crawling through Dak's head this morning, and he's unsure which he should responsibly scratch first.

The sound of a chair rolling across the linoleum makes Dak's head pop up like a prairie dog. He swivels his attention until his line of sight comes to rest on Legends. He has no clue how the kid had slipped past him. On any normal day, the guy was known to be the center of attention the moment he crossed the threshold.

Another itch to scratch. "*Legends.* You not gonna say, 'hi,' or '*toppa the mornin,*' or *anything?*"

The young detective turns that vacant gaze toward Dak. The lifeless look behind his bright eyes is becoming more and more concerning with each passing day. Dak's not sure if this is the manifestation of some sort of trouble at home, or with a lady, maybe a guy — *who knows* — maybe someone is sick? Dak has nothing but unsubstantiated theories. But whatever it is, it causes Dak plenty of worry.

"Sorry. Got a lot on my mind, I guess."

Dak laughs at that. Maybe the kid is okay, he thinks.

"Coulda fooled me, kid. You look like a zombie most mornings of late."

Legends doesn't laugh back, nor does he even crack a smile. He shrugs and turns his head back to the screen in front of him.

Any other day, any other person, and Dak would have taken personal offense to the behavior. But, this doesn't feel like the Legends he knows. Dak shrugs off the encounter as best he can, while simultaneously making the mental note to keep tabs on the kid.

Unsure of where to go next, Dak figures he might as well

call it a day. He thinks about reaching out to Ghini after seeing all the traffic issues from the day before, but he doesn't want to be a burden. More importantly, he isn't sure what to say. Her message was cryptic, and unfortunately, his gut is telling him that whatever is going on is much bigger than he can comprehend.

Before he closes his laptop and packs his bag, his eyes linger on the screen just long enough for something in the report to catch his eye. It reignites that burning itch of an idea that just won't seem to leave him alone

When you have eliminated every possibility, whatever's left, no matter how improbable, has got to be the answer...

Maybe, he's too close, and that's forced him into overanalyzing the whole thing? Or maybe he's too close and now he's losing his objectivity?

That sort of panicked ping-pong thinking is his cue to pack it up. There's not much else for him to do here, and more pressing is the fact that Dak needs a cigarette. Without, a second thought, he haphazardly packs up his bag and makes his way toward the exit.

But not before patting Legends on the shoulder, and wishing him a good day. He also tells the kid, "If ya need anything, I'm here for ya. Ya know that, right?"

Legends' slow movements deeply worry Dak. So too does the glossy eye contact and dispirited, *thank you*. It's incredibly odd behavior. But Dak's got that craving. Another itch. He's so close to getting his fix that nothing's going to get in the way of scratching this one quickly. He can spend time thinking about Legends with a cigarette in his hands if he needs to.

Dak exits the building into the back lot, where he sees another detective arriving for the day shift. Detective Mila Sommers. Married, mother of two, tough as nails, and a bit burly by Dak's standards. But she's the best at what she does, which is primarily fraud, larceny, and other non-violent crimes. And at the end of the day, that's the only thing that matters to him.

"Have a boge?" She calls over to him while sliding out of her beat-up old caddie.

Dak pauses, looks over to his ruddy old sedan that's also seen better days and decides the company sounds nice. "Read my mind."

He pulls out his own pack and saddles up next to her against the hood of her still-warm Cadillac. They sit in silence for some time before Dak looks over at her enjoying her *American Spirits*. She'll be here a while, so why not have a chat, he thinks. "You notice anything strange about Legends lately?"

"Fuck yeah I have." She says exhaling a large cloud of smoke. "Kid's been *real* weird lately. Reminds me of when The Captain got his heart broken by that two-timing little hussy."

Dak had forgotten about that little incident.

A few years back Captain Boone had been married to a woman that none of them ever met. Not entirely odd on its own, but it went on that way for nearly a decade. Then all of a sudden, he comes in one day, disheveled, looking like a zombie, and piss-drunk. Out of nowhere, he starts spewing into the bullpen that she had been cheating on him. Unfortunately, the show didn't end there. He proceeded to wail on about how she had told him that one of the kids wasn't even his. He'd retched in the middle of the floor after that. For the next month, Boone had been hardly more than a vegetable.

Fortunately, he pulled through.

Dak hopes Legends will too. The only difference is, everyone knows Legends isn't tied down. "Damn. Yeah, it is kinda similar."

"Except without the hot dog stains and snot bubbles." She

laughs through another cloud of grey smoke hovering on the warm morning air.

The squeal of rubber on asphalt alerts them to the arrival of another car pulling into the lot. This one's a patrol car, and the driver is a Uni who takes up two spots a few yards down from the smokers. With a brash sense of urgency, Officer Bradley exits the vehicle and is quick to make a bee-line for the building.

"Someone's in a hurry." Sommers chuckles. "What do you think she's got going?"

"Who knows? Could be anything. She didn't even turn off the cruiser. Doubt she even noticed us. At least, not moving like that."

"Oh, she definitely didn't. Maybe just really needed to drop the kids off at the pool." Sommers gives Dak an all-too-rough elbow to the ribs as she lets loose an iconic chortle. When she notices Dak practically keeling over, a hand plastered to his side, she throws in a child-like apologetic look.

Before either of them can address the levity of the playful exchange, Officer Bradley is back out the door with Legends in tow. It's been a while since Dak's seen that look on Legends' face. He looks determined and is moving with an air of urgency about him. The two are quick to get into the patrol car and whip out of the lot before either Sommers or Dak have a chance to ascertain the emergency.

As he wonders what could be up, Sommers taps him on the arm and leans in close. "How much you wanna bet those two are fucking?"

7

RISE AND SHINE

The knock at her door shatters the dream-like reality that Ghini had finally slipped into. Slow to recall her surroundings, and why she is there in the first place, Ghini is quick to pull the pillow over her head and drown out whoever is responsible for this egregious disturbance.

She hadn't slept well. Once she finally dozed off, that is. What sleep she had managed to attain, had been one of those toss-and-turn sort of nights. She wished she had asked for something to drink. She'd even considered taking a toke off their hosts' joint. But she was proud of herself for not doing so. Still, the faint echoes of her cravings linger into the morning. They whisper their lies from somewhere beneath the pillow.

It'll help you sleep.

It'll take the edge off.

It'll make it all easier.

Somehow, she has remained strong through all the falsities of her cravings and addictions, thus far.

In the course of all her desires, the strongest yearnings

came amidst the thundering knocks for her begotten Adderall. It's the best pick-me-up in her arsenal. The stimulant she is incapable of moderating, and why she is begrudgingly grateful she left it behind.

She pulls her head from behind the pillow only to realize that the world hasn't left its twilight period between the evening's darkness and the morning's light.

A wave of frustration leeches into her voice as she shouts, "*What?*"

"Ya decent?" Samuel's drawl comes through the door clearly.

She lets loose a groan that doubles as her confirmation that she is.

The door cracks enough for a mop of silver hair to poke through the opening. "Manny wants to take us over now. Observe how she reacts to the daylight. We're heading out in five."

She hears herself groan once more. But before she can complain, she employs some of that mind-over-matter ju-ju to spur herself onward. She needs to recapture the strength of that moment when she'd poured all her wine down the drain.

"Okay, I'll be out in two. There better be coffee."

Samuel is sure to let Ghini know, "It's already on the counter." The words drift out before the door closes lightly, behind a quiet chuckle.

Ghini's ready and dressed in a pair of jean shorts, combat boots, and a crewneck sweater before her two minutes are up. She surprises even herself with how quickly she manages to get herself together.

The morning is dark, but they're walking toward the first fragments of sunlight erupting on the horizon. Ghini enjoys watching the steam rise from her oversized coffee mug against the changing colors of the dawning sky.

Manny leads the way as they traverse the cool morning field. He mentions that Lawson is already at the trailer waiting for them.

Ghini has practically finished everything but the dregs at the bottom of the mug by the time they reach the distant trailer. Inside, Lawson asks everyone to take a seat. He's got a thermos that must be able to carry a gallon in volume. Its disproportionately small mouthpiece still billows steam into the bald brother's face as he takes his time sipping from the behemoth container.

In the silence of the space, Ghini takes the time to make a second inventory of the little trailer. The first thing she notices that she hadn't before, are all the books haphazardly strewn about. She sees Mary Shelly's *Frankenstein* predominately featured, but there are encyclopedias, magazine cutouts, and more horror novels than she cares to count. Old and new books alike, poke out from under the drapery of the couch. They're tucked behind the mason jars of marijuana, and even more form piles in the corners of the room. Strewn throughout are several notebooks and binders. Some have doodles, others don't. It's a hodgepodge of inconsistency.

Her diminished ability to focus on any one thing feels like it's something she should attribute to her Adderall withdrawal. Regardless, she wonders if this might be a good thing. She is taking in more of her surroundings, after all.

"Miss Ghini, are you with us?" She looks up, realizing all three men are staring. She's not sure what she's missed, if anything. To be courteous, she offers a polite nod, hoping Lawson takes the sign to mean he should continue. "Okay, we gotta set some ground rules here. Manny and I have always made it our mission to ensure that the two of us are never down there at the same time. She's got — screw it, Manny calls 'em *powers,* and that works. Specifically, she can hypno-tize ya."

He pulls up some off-brand smart tablet that Ghini's never seen before and turns it to them. On the screen is a video feed of a black and white concrete quarantine cell. At least that's what it looks like to Ghini. There is a metal toilet in one corner, and there are markings on the wall, but it's difficult to make anything out specifically. What ends up catching her eye, are the reinforced cinder blocks on the far walls. From which, huge, thick chains protrude. The links ebb downward into a mass of what looks like comforters, and that's when Ghini notes the lack of a bed in the cell.

"Is she in there?" Her finger hovers over the screen where the mass of comforters lies.

"Yup. She gets cold at night. She's gotta stay warm for survival."

"One of the first things she told us," Manny interjects. "Yeah, she talks to us. Honestly, it was creepy at first. Espe-cially since there wasn't much've a difference. She'd talk to ya like anyone else."

"But don't go making eye contact." Lawson quickly adds. "That's how she can get ya. We always make sure to keep her blindfolded, but if anything changes that, we don't go down there. The general rule of thumb is, never go down without first checking the cameras. Cuz if she's not wearing one, well, it's a process to get it on."

The comforter nest begins to stir on the screen, and silence envelops the group. A long slender arm with bony fingers bursts from the mass, and Ghini notes how sharp and barbed the nails of each finger look.

"Those are her stingers." Lawson stretches the screen to reveal an up-close look at the woman's hand. At first, the barbs don't seem to be apparent. Ghini thinks it might have been a trick of the screen, but she wasn't the only one to see them, so that can't be true. That's when they flap like the gills of a fish — in and out of her nails. It's easily noticeable on the tiny but stretched screen. Slight, needle-like things, hardly longer than an ant, or some other equally small insect.

Manny takes the tablet and adds, while pinching the screen back to its normal size. "See here, though. That's reinforced plexiglass. There's no way she's breaking through it. Her chains are mounted into the cement wall and reinforced with additional cinderblocks and concrete. She's strong enough to throw any one of us half a football field, but this set-up's worked nicely."

Ghini looks at the brothers, "Okay, let me get this straight you've had her down there for twenty years?" They nod in reply, waiting to see where she goes with this. "And there's never been a single accident? No escapes? No casualties? The pair of you look to be scar free, not to mention alive, so how have you managed so long?"

The two brothers share a near-identical and uncomfortable chortle. But it's Manny who takes the lead. "Well, see, we done had our problems over the years. Thr— Two instances in particular. The first time . . . *Lawson* had thankfully just purchased a tranq gun and had put a whole clip in her back before she got more than a hundred yards from the building."

"Took that much for her to drop."

"Sure did."

"The second time went a lot different." Lawson pauses. "She didn't *get out.*"

"*Instead,* she got to *me,*" Manny says, side-eying his brother. "We don't know how. I don't remember, and we hadn't installed the cameras yet. But I was watching her, and somehow she got me. She met my eyes and done turned me like the snake hair lady . . ."

"Medusa."

"Yeah, Medusa, thanks, Samuel."

Now Lawson interjects, "Thankfully, I can't let her go. That requires both of us. But she's cunning, always was. Yeup. So, I employ the less drastic of our safety measures and try to gas her. See these pipes here." He points at the screen, directing everyone's gaze toward several PVC pipes funneling out of the ceiling. "I can pump whatever gas I want through there, but I've learned to keep sleeping gas on hand as it seems to be the most effective in case of emergency."

"He tried to pump the gas through, but it'd been disconnected. Lawson left me downstairs and went around out back to the shed behind to try and inspect all the connections."

"I was already wary that she'd gotten to Manny, but wasn't ready to believe. Plus why would they not try to lure me downstairs? That's how she'd get me."

"Wait, how'd you know she could hypnotize you guys?" Ghini's quick to recognize the hole in their story.

Manny steps forward and waves his arms like he's falling backward. "That goes *way* back to when we first found her. She'd disappeared. Thought she'd run off with this particular white man. But then we hear she's at the bar down the road. So of course, we speed on over and find her with a group of ladies. Now our Momma wasn't known to have many lady friends, but it looked more like she was flirting with them than anything. The way they hung on her every word. And these weren't no strangers. They was other ladies from the res, and some of the townsfolk as well. All of whom had ran off that morning without warning, apparently.

"So we get there, and we accosts her." Manny has to demonstrate the shove he supposedly gave his mother. "We says, '*hey momma, what you doin' out here? Where ya been?*' But she rounds on us, and she pounces on me with those eyes.

They aren't all nest-like yet, but they are starting to change. If it weren't for Lawson, I think I'd have been done for, or maybe worse. But, yeah he . . ."

"Beat her over the head with a fire extinguisher. Then I turned it on and she stopped moving altogether once I'd covered her in the freezing foam." The younger brother pats his older brother on the back. "I didn't even see my own momma in that moment. I just seen my big brother in trouble, and that was something I couldn't allow."

There's a morbid silence in the air, and Ghini looks to Samuel, whose placid features let her know to hang tight a bit longer.

"So, I guess to answer your question, it was then that we knew. Cuz as we dragged her out, all the women that was with her followed along like little ducklings. They eventually snapped out of it several hours later. What we gathered from 'em was, they seen those eyes and then lost track of themselves. It was like they was only along for the ride. Her little playthings for the day."

Manny tags back in. "But the point of the *previous* story is that while Lawson was being the good brother — fixing' the gas — I was under Momma's spell. And . . . and, I did something I ain't proud of."

"I can tell it."

"NO... No, thanks, Lawson. I gotta own this." Despite that, his eyes burrow into the carpeting. "I went to the neighbors' and took they little girl. She weren't very old. Seven, maybe? I know I brought her back here. But when I came back to being myself, Lawson was shaking me. Struck me a couple times too. Just screaming, *'what've you done?'"* Manny pauses for a deep breath. "What I'd done was I'd fed that little girl to Momma. She killed her and ate her like a turkey dinner. Just prying and peeling . . ."

Ghini feels like she's going to send her coffee right back up and out. Quite possibly, pass out. Images of Jeannie flicker in her mind. Except, now she's in a cage. Like an animal. And she takes the form of the creature from the nightmares she's been having. Pincers and claws rip at the air. But now there's a bigger bug. And Jeannie's screaming. She's crying out through thick streams of tears, *Moms! Moms! Help! Help me, Moms!*

WHY AREN'T YOU HELPING ME, MOMS?

"Don't let it get to ya Miss Ghini," Manny says with a gentle smile. It is as if she has been sucked through a whirlpool back to the present.

As time passes, she begins to worry that such a vivid dream could only be a premonition. But Ghini could never believe such things. Or so she tells herself.

All three men are staring, and she does not care for it. She quietly lets them know she's okay, and after Lawson double-checks with her, he picks up where his brother had left off.

"We don't know nearly enough about them. But, what I can safely tell you both is, they're carnivores. They need meat, and over the years we've at least discerned that much. However, there is more and a lot of it is stranger than anything you could've imagined." It's clear Lawson is doing his best to re-direct his brother's survivor's guilt.

"Yeah, like even though that girl was fres . . ." Manny looks like a masochist at this point. His face twisted in a forlorn grin. As if he has accepted the need for the story to erupt out of his gut like an eighties sci-fi alien, if he's ever to find closure. "Momma prefers to let her meat rot. She'll eat only a tiny bit, and leave the remains in a corner for days before getting back to her leftovers.

"We've also found she can go a little over two weeks without food before she gets incredibly violent. We don't know how long she could actually go before starving. But her ruthless anger is not a pretty sight"

"She don't need water either. But she likes juices and sugary liquids. Like soda and sports drinks."

The talk of the creature's diet goes out the window when Ghini's head whips around. Something moved out of the corner of her eye, and now everyone's attention has fallen on the same spot. There, on the screen, the woman is up and about. Her gaze is locked on the camera. At least it appears that way. She has a thick, hefty blindfold across the upper half of her face.

Ghini doesn't believe herself crazy for believing the woman can see through it. The woman's sightline is perfectly fixed, not once interrupted. Not even the swaying movements of her body, as if she's listening to a song, following the rhythm, break her intense leer upon the camera.

"So, when is it usually warm enough for her to come out?" Ghini asks without any of them looking away from the screen.

"We had to confirm it a couple-a times, but we've got it pegged somewhere around sixty degrees." Lawson is quick to jump on this one.

"She do not like the cold." Manny tags back in. "She starts acting like a lush if her body temp drops too low. We thought we killed her one time because we let her go the whole night without anything but her underwear. Yet, she came back after snuggling up in some blankets for an entire day. These things, or at the very least our Momma, seem to be resilient."

"Sounds like it." Ghini's thoughts drift back to Jeannie. She and Manny have a lot in common, it seems. They both have it easy when it comes to falling into that dark spiraling abyss. She can't help but ask herself, *was Jeannie one of them now? Or had she just been a meal?*

Samuel rallies the group's attention. "What do ya feed her now?" His eyes pinch with the weight of an accusation.

Manny is very quick to pipe up with a response. "Well, we didn't keep her a secret from the tribal elders. They had stories for us, but once we'd asked enough questions, they'd formed their own answers. So, they didn't get us far. Confirmed a few things we already knew. Unfortunately, we've had to desecrate a few of the townsfolk's graves. None of the villagers know it was us. But those on the res, they've always known. And that's when they started moving out. They couldn't stand what we was doing, but it's my family!"

Lawson adds with a quick and uncomfortable chuckle, "Only problem was, she don't like it *too* spoiled. Always a picky woman."

Ghini and Samuel share an anxious glance with one another, knowing they don't like the sound of where this is heading.

"Does she not eat animals?" Ghini hears herself ask, dreading the response.

"She'll eat 'em if she's hungry enough." Manny turns off the tablet and tosses it toward the aging couch. "But she does have preferences. Seeing as it is feeding time after all, why don't the three of us go down there and let you see her up close? She ain't had visitors in some time, outside Lawson and me. I'm sure she'll appreciate it."

8

MOMMA

There is an uncomfortable anxiety in the air as Manny undoes the slew of deadbolts and menagerie of locks on the old oaken door.

Though, that feeling is nothing in comparison to the disquieting dread that rips through Ghini like a gale storm the moment Lawson returns each of them to their locked positions. The sounds echo into the dark and damp concrete stairwell that leads them down into the Earth.

When the stairs reach their end, they pour out into a nearly empty concrete landing. It was as if this room had been something at one point in time but had since been abandoned. There was damage to the concrete facade. Cracks in the cement flooring beneath their feet are abundant. Not to mention, the entire space is coated with the kind of dust that only accumulates from construction-type work.

Ghini thinks to ask where they are. She wants to ask a myriad of questions, but she'll settle on just the one plaguing her most.

"Why go through all this effort? Why not call the government, like the CIA or Men in Black type shit?"

Manny's body shakes with laughter as he turns to her. "Miss, you should know as well as I, why I ain't trust the government. Look around you." She follows his gestures circling the desolate room. This elicits another uncomfortable laugh. "Sorry, I mean *figuratively*. Look at where we live. Look at this skin. Hell, even Samuel'd get laughed out of the room, looking like broke Sam Elliot over here. No offense, Samuel.

"But, I mean, c'mon Ghini, let's be realists. What are they gonna do if I could convince them to believe me? If they actually did come here. They'd kill us all, including me, just to keep everything all hush-hush. As for momma, death would be the best-case scenario."

Is that selfish?

Ghini ponders that question silently. She knows the question plagues her because if she had to do the same for Jeannie, would she? She's never quite been one to trust the government herself. A smile flicks along her lips as she thinks of the ridiculousness of asking the government for help with something like this, and the Montoya brothers certainly would not have it any easier. Manny was right about that much.

As she searches for the words, Ghini notices another oaken door. It's darker than its predecessor, and she gets the impression — *thicker*. It has metal slats running up and down as well as side-to-side. *Reinforcements.* It feels like she is in a movie, on the precipice of going to meet the big bad supervillain tucked away in the state-of-the-art supermax prison.

A private meeting with a dubious Hannibal lector.

"Yeah, I guess you're right. This where we're going next?" She asks pointing to the door.

Manny nods and undoes several more deadbolts before ushering the three of them into another shadowy and musty concrete stairwell.

"This is the last one. I promise. Just . . . we have to be cautious. We can't make it easy for her if something should happen and she gets out."

"Why don't you lead the way."

They are the first words Samuel has uttered in some time, and though on paper it might look like a question, Samuel's tone is most certainly not an ask. He locks his arm against Ghini's sternum, preventing her from moving forward. His cold, husky-like eyes fall on Manny.

"Yeah, I guess I should?"

"Yes, yes ya should."

Manny looks uncomfortable as he waves his braid side to side across his back while snaking passed them to the fore-front of the group. This stairwell isn't as long but does have a hitch in it, making it darker and more foreboding.

Samuel doesn't say a word, but as he puts his first foot on the next step, he lifts his shirt to reveal two pistols on his back waistband. He stands there waiting, and Ghini, who certainly speaks Samuel, can translate what he's conveying in an instant — *time is of the essence.*

Spend enough time around Samuel Clemens, and you will get to know his nonverbal cues with ease.

Still, she doesn't feel comfortable with either of the two firearms in her possession. He's got some sort of policeman's type Glock, or whatever, that she does not want to touch. Unfortunately for her, there's not a lot in this world that she trusts more than Samuel Clemen's instincts. Begrudgingly, she assumes responsibility for the smaller .22 revolver. She quickly, and cautiously, slides the weapon from his waistband to hers.

As they maneuver down the staircase, Ghini fixates on the damp smells and musty air that reach out and claw at her senses from somewhere in the darkness. The atmosphere of the space worms its way into her mind, forever etching itself into her memory. She pictures the walls, nothing more than relatively thin layers of rock holding back the entire pressure of the Earth wanting to fall in on itself. Her nerves are palpable and whisper dark thoughts to her about how this place could cave in on them at any second. Entombing them with a monster, if not a terrible death.

The scent of dirt permeates the space with a weighty aroma that makes her feel ever the more vulnerable down in this hillbilly bunker, or prison, or whatever term the brothers chose to use. The only thing keeping her moving right now is the sense of security she feels behind Samuel.

As they step out onto another concrete landing, Ghini quickly assesses this newest room. Its space is lit with a handful of long fluorescent lights that hum an unnatural rhythm in this artificial space.

Manny is looking up toward the camera when his mother crashes into the plexiglass with enough force to send plumes of dirt flaking from the concrete ceiling above. Her eyes are hidden behind the thick blindfold that strangely complements her deep mahogany skin.

"Hi, momma." Manny briefly glances in the woman's direction before darting his eyes toward Ghini and Samuel, who stand in comparable shock.

Up close, it's clear that the woman doesn't look like she's aged. Ghini would peg her to be around her mid to late thirties. Mostly due to the lack of blemishes on her near-pristine skin.

On the other hand, *she's a monster*.

Her frame appears warped. All of her curves are angles. Bony, cartilaginous, defined angles. Everything from her jaw to her elbows, knees, hips, and ankles looks sharp and pointed.

"I've taken some precautions that Lawson doesn't know about to ensure she isn't able to get that blindfold off, but you just never know. So, I'd recommend always averting your gaze or being ready to do so."

Manny sighs moving towards the cage. But his eyes wander back to the ceiling. Everything about this gives Ghini the *heebie-jeebies.*

It's that trust.

She doesn't feel like she trusts any part of this situation. Samuel had given her the pistol for a reason, and he'd brought her here for a purpose. The latter part has been very much accounted for, but she's concerned overall with where Samuel's trust meter stands with the Montoya brothers.

"Uh, Manny. You called her eyes nest-like earlier. What'd you mean by that?"

There had been a fragile silence in the room, and Manny looks relieved like he can breathe again, now that the dense veil of quiet has been torn through. "Have you not seen their eyes?"

Ghini shakes her head and pulls out her phone. "Not clearly, I don't think." She turns the phone to Manny who pinches the screen and zooms in on the image of The Dop in the convenience store. The picture that had started her down this increasingly terrifying rabbit hole. But as he does, he slices his fingertip on the cracked glass.

"*Fuck.*" He yelps, but doesn't pull his gaze from the screen. "Yup, that's them. Wait a sec. She kinda looks like . . . *you* . . ." The phone falls from his hand and performs a tiny hop and skip as it cracks further against the concrete floor.

The room feels frigid in an instant. As if all the warmth had just been vacuumed from it. The men feel it too. They're both quick to pull pistols. Manny's aimed at Ghini, and Samuel's aimed at Manny. Neither man fires, thankfully. But the tension between the three of them starts Ghini shaking violently with adrenaline. So much so, she doesn't think she'd even be capable of holding her own weapon if she could get a hand on it.

"Clemens?"

"Yeah, Manny?"

The room feels like it's only getting colder. The woman in her plastic cage is breathing heavily against her container walls. Fogging the space with an expression that almost looks like fevered excitement.

"What did you bring into my house? What are you, Samuel? Man? Or servant?"

Ghini looks at Samuel, expressing her discomfort with the predicament. But his grey eyes say that he has the current situation under control.

"Manny, I see this predator down here and it very much feels like *I'm* in the den of the beast. I ain't setting foot in such a place without a little protection."

"Clemens. These . . . *things* . . . they ain't protection. They're *monsters!* And you done brought another one down here. She'll kill us both."

"What are you talking about?" He looks at Ghini, and the way his eyes squint, helps Ghini figure it out a hair faster than Samuel.

"Oh shit! *Wait wait wait wait . . . wait!*" Her hands fly upward and as quickly as she can, Ghini points a finger toward the *thing* in the cage. "You think . . . I'm one of *those?*"

Manny nods. His eyes narrowed as well.

Ghini doesn't know if she wants to laugh, or cry, or collapse, but she's definitely relieved.

"She's not one of 'em. But her daughter might be."

And there it is. Someone's finally said it. Jeannie might be a monster.

9

CHIYE

The tension in the room is at its pinnacle. They are all one second away from crossing the breaking point.

Ghini isn't sure how to react. Her heart feels like it has just been forcibly torn in two, but she is also looking at *the thing* that her daughter may have become. Or even *fed*.

No, can't think that way.

Samuel looks forlorn. As if he'd just brought a soldier's family the folded flag that they had always feared would return. But the look on Manny's face is indignant. Like he can't decide whether to be furiously angry or woefully sad.

"God . . . mother f— I hate you Samuel."

"Swear it. She aint one."

A defeated sigh precedes, "I know she ain't. It's just — *FUCK*." He lowers his firearm and looks up at the camera in the corner. The lens appears fixed on the mother monster, and from what Ghini remembers of the tablet, she believes Manny should be in frame. However, she's not sure Samuel and she are. In fact, Ghini has an air of confidence filling her lungs that assures her they are safely excluded from the video feed.

"What's going on here Montoya?"

Manny's features go a bit feral. He looks like he might lash out at any second, tight-roping that thin wire between fear and reck-lessness. "I . . . *FUCK!*" He starts muttering to himself and Samuel ushers Ghini backward so that he is between her and Manny.

Her hand now moves back to the pistol. What had seemed so small and about as menacing as a BB gun, now feels like the button for nuclear Armageddon against her palm. She can feel herself trembling, despite knowing how warm it is down here.

"Family's all I got."

"Pardon?" Samuel keeps trying to shoo Ghini behind him, but she can't help herself from peering around his hip like a curious toddler. And what she sees is a single tear trailing down the slope of Manny's cheek. It's out of place for the big man. It feels like the wrong emotion for the situation.

He brushes the droplet away. "Ghini. You asked why we ain't go to the government? Truth is, I was raised to believe family's all we got. And even if all my family's monsters, I'm still gonna love 'em."

"Manny? What're you saying?"

Manny's quick. His pistol hand flies upward, and Samuel rounds on top of Ghini. His arms wrap around her waist, and he takes her to the ground like an all-pro linebacker. Though, he makes certain to cradle her head, preventing dangerous contact with the concrete.

Ghini on the other hand has the opposite reaction. Rather than run, her adrenaline has kicked in with a fight response. On instinct, her hand flings around Samuel, pointing the little pea shooter at Manny. But, just as she feels her finger begin to squeeze the trigger, is when Samuel's shoulder buries into her sternum.

BANG!

BANG!

Two distinct shots, fired by two different weapons, echo throughout the chamber.

Samuel is on top of Ghini, who's had the wind knocked out of her, but is otherwise okay. "Samuel! Samuel! Are you okay?" She screams.

Samuel tentatively lifts his head and pushes himself above her so she can see him. The blood dripping from the bullet wound that she expects to be in the center of his chest isn't there.

"You okay?"

She nods and scrambles to peer around Samuel. The gun had slipped from her hand when she'd hit the floor, and her fingers now erratically search to regain control of the weapon.

But, she freezes at the sight of Manny. He's aimed above them. She follows the muzzle's line of sight to see that it is pointed toward the camera on the ceiling.

That's when her worst fears drop a pit wide open within her. She's shot Manny. She's killed someone.

Except, she hasn't.

Thankfully, he's unscathed, not a single speck of blood dripping from a tiny pin-sized wound on his chest that doesn't exist.

Samuel sees the look on Ghini's face and turns to Manny, with a worried look of confusion.

"The camera. Lawson can't see this."

"I thought you were gonna kill us!" Ghini shouts around Samuel.

Samuel quickly bear crawls from atop her, before helping Ghini to her feet.

"Talk Montoya." Samuel scolds the man, who looks more

like a robust small child who has ended up in a man's body during one of those body-swapping movies.

"Listen. There ain't goin' to be a lot of time here. Lawson will be on his way soon. I can't do this no more though. So, we're getting the pair of you outta here."

"What are you talking about?" Ghini snaps at him. The confusion is maddening and her emotions are racing the gamut at record pace.

"There's no time."

"Make time."

"*Ghini*. What *are* you doing?" Samuel croaks.

She grabbed the gun on instinct just a second ago and has now trained it on Manny. She doesn't trust a word the man says. She needs answers. They've come all this way, been given a taste of Pandora's Box, and now it's open. She won't trust anyone who refuses to give her a straight answer.

"*Now*. Manny. I don't hear your brother. So, if you're scared . . . *fine*. But you're telling us what we want to know. If this is some kind of stunt, I won't hesitate to put a bullet through your fat fuckin' head! *This is about my baby!*" She screams the words with such fierce rage, it lights a fire that scorches adrenaline through her. She's ready to take on the world and do whatever's necessary.

Only a second or two passes from Ghini's war cry to the sound of a single *thump* above them.

Manny goes pale, and Samuel has said something to Ghini, but her eyes, ears, and mind are all trained on one thing. *Manny*. The man whose eyes sit baseball-sized in his skull, darting with plea after plea.

"Talk quickly." She doesn't flinch, but when Samuel lays a hand on her forearm, she unleashes a glare as sharp as daggers through him. That's his cue to back off a step, but he still remains close.

"Just put the gun down, Ghini." Manny whines.

"You're wasting time. Talk."

Manny resembles less and less a man, and more and more a scared child, who may or may not have a desperate need to use the toilet.

There's a growing commotion above them, but it doesn't seem as if Lawson's down the first stairwell yet.

"Okay, fine. Fine. I'll talk, but please back away from the door."

Samuel starts moving, while Ghini remains rooted to her spot. He gives her a tug on the collar, and she begrudgingly lets him steer her backward. She doesn't flinch with any step. She keeps every part of herself trained on Manny. She has an implicit trust that Samuel's doing what's best for her. However, that doesn't mean she must turn away from the man ahead of her.

"Everything I told you was true. But it wasn't me that Momma got that second time. And it wasn't me in the bar. If you knew more than you were lettin' on, I assumed you might recognize the signs and figure out about Lawson."

A thundering crash lets the group know that the first big oaken door is open. It shakes the entire subbasement with the force generated from striking the wall above.

"Go on." She sees he wants to stop, but she refuses to let him.

"Lawson's a *drone*. A servant to Momma. Hypnotized by her eyes. He'll only obey *her* unless she tells him otherwise. He's got some strength that ain't quite normal, but it's more like he lacks inhibition. If she tells him to do something, he'll do it. He'd walk across hot coals without flinching if she told him to."

The next door swings open, and the room shakes again. The footsteps are slow and gradual though. He's in the final stairwell now. They can hear Lawson's hefty footsteps echoing in the concrete walls. Every eye is trained on the exit way situated between Ghini and Manny. When the first boot strides from out of the stairway's shadows, Ghini almost squeezes the trigger.

"Lawson! Brother, what're you doing? You can't break the rules. You know that. Momma wouldn't like it."

The younger brother stops and turns toward Manny in silence. With her sightline to Manny blocked, Ghini can only see what's beyond him. Behind, and to his left, is the plastic cage that contains his — *mother*. On the opposite wall, is a collection of jars filled with items and fluids. It's like something out of a cheap haunted house. One looks like it has a pair of eyeballs suspended in whatever chemical is preserving them. Another, some sort of internal organ, there might be a tongue in the one next to that. There are several with what appears to be just a fluid of some sort. It looks more viscous than whatever formaldehyde-type preservative is in the other jars. Its color is different too. To Ghini, they look like jars of watered-down honey.

"Brother, no. *Stop!*" Manny shouts, and Ghini's gaze drops back to the duo ahead of her. Lawson is no longer distracted by his brother. His gaze has now fallen on the creature in the cell.

Once more, Ghini watches the woman. It's unsettling the way her head lolls back and forth. Behind the blindfold, her sightline looks to be darting from her younger son to Ghini and Samuel like a pendulum. It is not a human movement.

Lawson no longer looks like the jovial man they'd met earlier. This person in front of them appears soulless. Flat. Blind to the world, all its beauty and consequences. He takes a step and Ghini fires. She sees Manny dive toward the see-through cell to get out of the way. But her shot hits Lawson directly in the shoulder. A trickle of blood turns into a tiny puddle under his collarbone, but his stride doesn't falter. He takes a couple more steps, and Ghini fires shot after shot. Each one forces an anxious panic to ring through her. She can feel her hands beginning to shake and succumb to the recoil of each shot.

She grazes his ribs and buries one in the meat of his thigh, but he keeps meandering forward, unimpeded. The rest of her shots don't find a home on the man's body, which only serves to frustrate and rattle her.

"Ghini, *get* down!" Samuel wraps his left arm around the back of her waistline and pulls her in an arc around his left side. With his right hand, he pulls the large pistol, which he'd recovered while moving Ghini earlier. He takes aim and plants a large caliber bullet in the center of Lawson's forehead. There's a crack, crash, and *thump* in quick succession as the expressionless man crumples backward mid-stride.

While Ghini and Samuel check on one another, Manny runs to his brother's side. The distress on his face is clear as day as he rests a hand across his brother's brow.

"I'm sorry Lawson. But you are no longer a witch's tool. You are free. And one day, I will see you, and all the ancestors, and we will . . . we will sing once more." He rests his own forehead on that of his brother's, never mind the vicious gaping hole. Slumped there, he whispers something that neither Ghini nor Samuel can discern, but it feels as if that is the proper way of things.

When Manny gets to his feet, he has a splotch of red viscera across his forehead, but he does nothing with it. "I cut out her eyes, and when that didn't work, I cut out her tongue. But he still remained her slave." The nonchalant manner of his sudden statement worries Ghini.

Samuel however, seems unfazed as he steps forward. Once

again placing him in the position of Ghini's shield. "I'm sorry about your brother Manny, but —"

"No buts. It was the right thing to do." His face shows nothing but steeled emotion. The hurt is there, but so evidently locked away behind tense eyes and a clenched jaw. "He was her prisoner for life. She stopped being my Momma a long time ago. Or maybe, I stopped being her son. But I was always Lawson's brother, and his big brother at that. His *chiye.*"

An eerie *creeeeeeak* steals everyone's attention. There at the entrance to the cell is the creature, moving her way across the open threshold. The door had cracked open after being hit with an errant shot from Ghini's weapon earlier. The creature's head is cocked to the side, and she holds her limbs high like a praying mantis. Her movements are harsh and erratic. Tense, but swift. She lets out a throaty, yet guttural squawk-type sound that reaps through the three bystanders.

"She can't hypnotize us, right? Right?" Ghini's urgency is unlike anything she's ever known. "C'mon Manny. We're good . . ."

"Let's go Ghini." Samuel takes her hand and trains his sights on the thing taking timid, almost birdlike stabbing steps toward their host.

Ghini does not need to be told twice, but apparently, Manny does. "C'mon Manny. We gotta *go.*" She wants to take a step toward grabbing the man, but Samuel restrains her with a firm hand clasped across her shoulder. Digging his fingers in, he continues to pull her backward.

"Nah. Momma, and I got some things we need to discuss."

"Manny! No! You've gotta come with us." Ghini's trying with all her might to break Samuel's grip, but his hands are large and his fingers are digging into her collar so sharply, that she doesn't have much choice, except to relent to being pulled behind him. He uses his full body to box her out of the room and into the stairwell.

"*Samuel.*"

"Montoya."

"Do not let her out. Ya hear me? Don't you fuckin' dare." He reaches into his pocket and throws a set of keys at Samuel. "Tiny green one's a skeleton key for every lock. Hit 'em all behind you, and when you get upstairs . . ." Manny is interrupted by that same throaty hiss as before, but it's louder and the creature looks angrier. Though she's gaunt and bent, she stands a head taller than her son, with tense features.

The thing bends over and maneuvers her head next to Lawson's motionless body. There is a quiet, almost whimper-like sound before she stands up to her full height, much taller than before, and screams into her eldest son's face.

"Hi Momma."

Ghini ignores every frightened instinct in her body to run. She desperately wants to bull her way past Samuel, but he won't budge a millimeter. Instead, he's still worming her into the stairwell, with nowhere to go but up.

Unfortunately, as the screech ends, Ghini's heart sinks to the floor. The creature's giant slender hand rips through the back of Manny's shirt, spilling viscera and splatter in every which direction. She lets out another scream, like a war cry.

It's now that Manny utters what Ghini knows will be his last words. "Upstairs . . . Take the big yellow notebook . . . The one with the honeycombs drawn on it . . . And . . . Push the red button . . . Next to the entry."

It's Manny's turn to let out a ferocious and thundering scream as he manages one final act of throwing his weight forward, and Ghini feels like she'll be sick as she hears the monster's arm move further through her eldest son.

Samuel, on the other hand, is quick to act. He grabs a fire

extinguisher from next to the doorway. It's only a little white one, but he thrusts it into Ghini's arms and hurries her up the stairs. The sounds of ripping and crunching below ring into the passageway. Ghini tries to focus on her pounding heart rather than the horrid images catapulting through her imagination.

Samuel pushes her across the threshold to the first basement landing, grabs the large oaken door, and slams it shut. Ghini's shaking. Her survival instincts have switched from fight to flight, and she needs to be out of this claustrophobic hellscape.

Back in the trailer, they lock the door quickly and barricade it with the heavy recliner.

Just as they feel a minor sense of security, they hear the thundering hammers of the creature below. They can only hazard a guess, but it feels pretty safe to say, she's going at that mid-level door. Ghini doesn't want to sit around waiting to see if it's going to hold up. She goes to look for the notebook amidst all the piles and piles of books and finds a thick five-plus section notebook with tattered edges, tabs, and what appear to be several coffee spills.

Samuel finds the button, which is only visible now because the recliner had been concealing the faded round object. It's one of those old-school fire alarm buttons for big gymnasiums, but the brothers had taped over the word extinguisher, so it just reads, *FIRE*.

"Ghini, you got the book?" She lifts it up to show him. "Good, get outside. *NOW.*"

"*What about you?*" Her voice strains.

"Don't worry bout me. I'm right on your coattails." He slams his hand into the button, and sprints toward the door. The old man is quick and light on his feet, rushing out right behind her into the humid morning air, which comes as a welcome relief.

Outside, they first hear the whistle of gas escaping, coming from beneath the trailer. There are multiple gasses, however. Ghini can tell because she's seen this at the Coke plant. The way the vapors don't mix in the air is something she witnesses all the time. Then comes the toxic pesticide scent, followed by the noxious fumes of propane gas.

The ground shakes beneath their feet as a muffled *WHUMPF* erupts below. Both Ghini and Samuel fall to the ground, and neither moves. Samuel keeps his pistol trained on the door, which is leaking dark black smoke into the mix. Meanwhile, Ghini aims the nozzle of her tiny fire extinguisher from just behind Samuel.

There, they wait frozen, expecting a throaty scream to come for them any second.

10

HEROES?

Dak hadn't seen either Legends or Bradley when he had clocked in for the night. But, he'd certainly heard about them. The entire building was buzzing with the news of their afternoon standoff.

Apparently, Bradley had gotten a tip from someone inside the rumor mill that a witness had been up for an early morning run and nearly got side swept by a passing vehicle. The man behind the wheel was a large individual from her neighborhood, driving a pickup truck with a young woman sleeping in the front seat. It was early and the witness had not thought anything of it. Simply, a couple coming home late. Then our witness goes on vacation and comes back to the news of the disappearance that had rocked the Black Hills.

Sounds like a great vacation to Dak, because the witness hadn't been up to date on any of the local news while out of town.

So, when they get back and see all the news stories, she goes and tells a neighbor who knows someone who knows someone who knows Bradley, and that is why the two had been in such a hurry the other day.

As it turns out, unlike so many other tips, this intel was good. They found a man by the name of Todd Dexter.

Dexter apparently had put up a fight, though. Managed to fire off an entire clip. Thankfully, only one found its mark, and it ended up being nothing serious, having clipped Legends in the shoulder. It was not anything that a few stitches and time would not be able to heal. Unfortunately, the suspect had already taken the life of another hostage, later identified as Maria Rios.

In the end, with her partner down, and backup still en route, Bradley put one between the creep's eyes. Thankfully, before Dexter was capable of doing any more harm to the officers or the Kalisch girl.

Dak hadn't even bothered trying to get the girl's statement when he had arrived at the hospital. She seemed to be in shock and wasn't the least bit surprised to learn that the family had wanted Legends and Bradley to do it.

With morning in full effect, the pair should have wrapped things up by now, over at the hospital, where both the Kalisch girl and Legends were evaluated.

Other than the brief excursion to the hospital, Dak's night had been quiet until now. As daylight continues to dawn, the heroes return, and it's a heroes' welcome they receive.

Dak remembers watching Legends' first National Championship game at South Dakota State. Despite a broken clavicle while scoring the winning touchdown, he celebrated with his teammates. When that kid had won, he was about as restrained and bashful as a wild hyena. The way he just galloped around the stadium, grinning, laughing, and hollering into the stands, getting the fans on their feet. It was like watching a rock concert.

This Legends is not the same. Dak finds himself failing to clap along with his fellow officers as the heroes' arrival envelops the bullpen. He's too far gone down a rabbit hole. Lost in thought. Because the Legends before him almost appears — *bashful* — modest even. Of course, he's not that same nineteen-year-old kid. Still, it is not the hero he has seen before. Jontay Legends' behavior continues to be — *off*.

All of this feels wrong. His cop gut isn't sitting right with this. Dak thinks about what Detective Sommers said the other day, *"How much you wanna bet those two are fucking?"*

Would that explain it?

Dak doesn't think so. Legends is a young guy; intelligent, with a good moral compass. But, he's still a young guy. Dak's seen the kid bragging about past flings with other women, including officers. Dak has been witness to the kid scrolling through his phone, highlighting the social media pictures of his most recent flings on many occasions. Dak wasn't one to frequent those conversations himself, but even he had to admit, if there's a scantly clad woman on a screen, there's a fifty-fifty chance that he's going to look.

Officer Bradley is a beautiful woman in her own right. She's no model or movie star, but she's always had clear skin, bright eyes, and kept fit. All are typically a plus in almost any man's book. On top of that Dak has noticed how the officer does appear to have slimmed down a bit these last few weeks. All this to say, Dak is certain there'd have been some slip of the tongue, some braggadocios lapse in judgment if the two were, in fact, an item.

So, he's not sure what is going on, but something is definitely up. For now, Dak is simply of the mindset that whatever it is, is not sexual in nature.

As people begin settling down, and the line forms to offer daps, pats, pounds, and shakes to the two heroes, Dak regains his seat. He's back to looking at what *he* has been investigating.

Todd Dexter
Age 44
Coca Cola Plant

He has those three things written down.

Dexter is close enough to Ghini's age that they'd likely be contemporaries, and sure enough, a quick call to the plant reveals that not only did he work the same shift as her, but the same floor. Increasing the likelihood that the two would have, at the very least, interacted, if not known each other on a personal level. Social media confirms a relationship between the two. They were indeed friends. She *laughed at* and *loved* many of his posts. His feed, on the other hand, was also littered with shares regarding Jeannie's disappearance.

Now two things about this worry Dak immensely.

The first elicits itself at the sight of a photo on the man's social media timeline. His profile is tagged to a picture of a man in a black polo and pants, with a clipboard. He's clearly coaching a group of teenagers on the rec center basketball court.

That's when Dak realizes that he had met Dexter on several occasions.

The Police Union sponsored the AAU team that the man coached for Christ's sake. Not to mention, how difficult it was to miss the giant known as 'Coach Todd.' But that was how Dak had always referred to the man, *Coach Todd*. He'd never learned the guy's last name. At least, if Dak had, he'd somehow failed to put two-and-two together that Todd Dexter and Coach Todd were the same person.

Thinking more about the man, Dak began placing him at several search parties for Jeannie. He'd stood there while Johnson had given directions and organized volunteers on multiple occasions.

They'd shaken hands!

What kind of judge of character was Dak, himself, if he could shake a cold-blooded murderer's hand and not once ever realize? *Some cop gut,* he thinks.

And two, which is significantly more disquieting, *what if that bastard also had something to do with Jeannie?*

It would not be the first time a serial killer immersed themself in an investigation. How many bodies would they find along the way?

"Good morning Detective Johnson." Dak spins in his chair to find Legends standing to his right. Once again, moving as quietly as ever, but he's got a juvenile grin across his face.

"Well, it seems you are in better spirits this morning. Surprising for a guy who just got shot."

"I've had plenty worse. Plus, I have to act happy. That is what you are supposed to do when you save someone's life. People are supposed to see you happy."

As quickly as Dak had thought the kid was getting back to normal, it seems that he is moving backward just as swiftly. Though, Dak's not entirely certain that this isn't a cry for help. Maybe the kid's depressed. Happens to plenty of guys on the force. Shit, Dak's had his ups and downs. He's got a good shrink though — when he needs it. Which isn't often, anymore, but Dak's never afraid to call if the occasion truly demands.

"You alright Legends? I'm sure the Captain would under-stand if you need time—"

"No time like the present." Bradley blows through and

saddles up next to Legends. "Detective Johnson." She offers a curt, but seemingly respectful nod.

"Where're the blues Officer?"

"That's Detective now." She's got a smirk that reminds Dak of the Cheshire Cat. It's nowhere near as wide, but it would glow in the dark menacingly along with her light-colored eyes.

"Congratulations, *Detective* Bradley. I'll buy you a round when you get off tonight. I'm off the next two nights anyhow."

"Tonight's not good." Her eyes linger a tad long, or maybe Dak's do. Because it looks like he's starting to see double when Officer Paradiso claps Legends on the back. Everyone blinks, and now that his eyes feel moisturized, Dak notices that his vision seems to have corrected itself. Everyone's eyes have the proper number of pupils.

"Legends! Superstar Quarterback! Superstar Detective! What can't this man do?"

"I couldn't do anything. It was Bradley who did everything and told me what to do."

Dak doesn't miss the flicker of annoyance that bolts across Bradley's face before she fiercely grabs Legends at the elbow and says, "We have to go. Got a lot to do. Goodbye, Detective. Goodbye, Officer."

Legends doesn't even offer a too-da-loo or a wave. He just does the old Irish Goodbye and walks off like a sled dog pulling its master.

Paradiso is left standing and confused. But before Dak can figure out his own excuse to get away, the officer fixes his attention on the detective. "Odds on those two bumping uglies? I'd say, *high.*"

Dak shrugs off the man's suggestion and looks down at his desk. There are his notes and copies of the crime scene report.

"I don't know, Paradiso," he says without looking up from

the paperwork. "But, I'm betting we missed something at old Dexter's place. Where's Officer Tomlinson?"

Paradiso rolls his eyes, the big man deflates at feeling passed over. "He's on FML. Something about an aunt or someone in Florida. I don't remember." He gives a cowardly side-eye toward Dak as he adds, "but I'm available if ya need a hand. . ."

The officer has a wanting and pathetic look about him. It reminds Dak of a movie where John Malkovich plays that "special" guy, named Lennie. The one who wants to hear his buddy talk about the rabbits.

Despite his contempt for Paradiso, and the officer's annoying presence, Dak knows that four eyes are always better than two, even if two of them belong to Victor Paradiso. If only he could have picked Tomlinson's brain about Legends, but there's no time for wishes and dreams.

"Alright, Paradiso. Saddle up. We're gonna go check out a crime scene."

11

EAVESDROPPING

Kari feels exhausted. The same kind of debilitating exhaustion that shows its teeth that second morning of a gnarly two-day hangover.

Her mind is as foggy as the Black Hills on a cool autumn morning. Only bits and pieces of the landscape are visible, the same way only small portions of her mind seem to be poking through the mental fugue.

Her surroundings are a primary focus to help reground her. There's Mel again. *Again?* It is quite strange to see Mel here for . . . for . . . she's not sure. She wants to say, for the *second* straight morning, but that sure does not seem right. It's like Deja Vu. Like she has run this gamut of thought patterns multiple times. She knows that sounds silly and attributes it to her mental fog. She half wants to ridicule herself for such a thought.

It might be possible that she is going through some sort of metamorphosis. Queenie certainly has been. At first, Kari had ignored it. Attributing it to a trick of the light, or that she'd simply overlooked some physical features about Queenie.

Except, there is not a single doubt in Kari's mind that Queenie has grown. It cannot be more than two inches, maybe three at most. But it's noticeable how she now towers over Kari. That is when her mother is not crouching down, which she does often now, trying to hide her lengthening appearance. In fact, everything about her appears stretched out. As if the muscle and fat hadn't grown with her. Instead pulled apart and kneaded like dough.

Looking at her, a stranger would think that she was not eating. At this point, her mother is nearing the epitome of *skin-and-bone*. Except, Kari knows Queenie to be well-nourished. The pair often eat at least one meal together each day. Then there are the frequent visits Queenie makes to her private chambers. Every daughter of Queenie knows that their mother is never to be disturbed while in there, but Kari is *well aware* that many of her sisters have heard the grunting and chomping echo from that back cavity. However, she cannot recall having ever seen a single spec of food brought back there.

She is certain that at some point she had tried going to the chamber herself. Maybe only once, but the memory is hazy, and all Kari can recall is being scolded away before ever reaching the entrance. Once more, Kari just wants to attribute it to the fog slowly meandering through her mind this morning and move on. Something, a memory, or a recollection, has to come out of it eventually.

Incidentally, Kari worries about the state of her mind. She may need to speak with Queenie about it if this persists. There's no telling what sort of condition she might be dealing with. It could be the first of its kind. Maybe it's a cold, and they are just affected differently.

Regardless, she can't let her mind speculate and spiral. She desperately wants to continue eavesdropping on her mother and Mel. The latter recently dismissed Kari from the chamber where they are currently holding a private conversation.

She hears the breath before the words even escape her sister's lips. "What're y —"

Kari springs backward and manages to swiftly clasp her hand over Willow's mouth. She looks different in her pantsuit. But there is no time to think about that. Kari knows they have been heard, it's only a matter of, whether or not Queenie and Mel do anything about it.

Kari holds her breath feeling a sense of anticipation. It's a dreadful experience that flutters away after only a few seconds that stretch on for a lifetime. Bradley's eyes betray an eerie curiosity as if she's inspecting Kari, who can't bring herself to turn around toward the chamber's entrance.

A brooding fear whirls around Kari's insides, providing unsubstantiated notice that Queenie, or worse, *Mel* is standing right there. But time manages to move on, and no one comes out of the chamber.

As if sensing the descending tension, Willow wraps a tight grip around Kari's fingers, patiently, yet forcefully easing off the appendages plastered across her mouth. Both women flip their eyes as they meet within the silence. It's not quite a language that they're developing, but the entire sisterhood — at least the older siblings — have more control over their eyes' micro-movements. Those little tells and twitches are capable of communicating volumes without so much as a huff or sigh.

The conversation between the two women plays out wordlessly, but they both gather the gist from one another.

Why were you crouching here, eavesdropping?

Isn't it obvious?

No. Tell me.

Fine. Listen.

Kari points to the room and Willow snakes up alongside the wall to get closer to the conversation.

"Are you sure you don't want me to send someone else to escort them my *likkle* scarlet joy?"

"Yes, my Queenie."

"We could send Detective Willow. It would make sense, and we could then take Mr. Legends out for a test drive alongside her. They'd give the move more credibility, don't you think?"

"I think it would until it comes to the attention of the precinct that their two hero detectives escorted the family into a disappearing act. I think that might raise an eyebrow or two. Especially, if there are parties who know about us."

"Do you think anyone knows about us?"

Willow and Kari exchange glances.

We should go.

No.

"*Think?* One-hundred percent. There's no way there isn't *someone* out there who knows about us."

Kari.

Don't move.

"But as far as someone, *actively* hunting us. I don't think we have our own Van Helsing yet. That isn't to say, he doesn't exist."

Queenie interjects, "All legends are based on fragile truths."

"What?"

"I read that somewhere, I think. But, it works here."

"Of course, my Queenie. However, I do think we should handle things as covertly and indiscreetly as possible. With a hat on, I'm just another little girl."

"Oh my no, you are so much more, my — "

"*Likkle* scarlet one. I know. But, I do believe I would be most useful on this task. It's taken us longer to create this window than I would like to admit, thanks to Sierra's hospitalization and all the media coverage. So, it'll be best that we get them out of here while those eyes are drawn elsewhere thanks to Bradley and Legends. Who, no, has not emerged yet, but we should be right around the twelve-hour mark now."

"You can just read my mind sometimes. I'm very proud of you Mel. You are a beautiful and intelligent being."

Go. Kari. Seriously.

Not happening.

"Thankfully, you are not my only intellectually capable daughter. I do believe I heard Willow out there, patiently waiting for us to finish our conversation."

FUCK.

Relax. Willow lightly pats Kari across the shoulder before turning the corner for the chamber.

"Good morning mother."

"Good morning you wonderful Willow! You are prepared to take custody of Detective Legends for the day?"

"I am."

"Then?"

"Detective Legends and I will go about our normal work day, before adjourning back to our respective homes. In the morning we will hold a press conference with the national affiliate to discuss the Kalisch Investigation. The Kalischs will, unfortunately, be indisposed and unable to make the event.

"However, this is when Velvet, *er*, I mean, Mel will escort the Kalischs to you for assimilation. After which, we will then move on to phase two, which—"

"We don't need phase two right now hon. Thank you Willow, I have complete trust in you for the day ahead. Mel, I believe we have covered *everything*? Good. I won't be needing anything else from you. So, until tomorrow my lovely daughters. Please be safe."

In unison the women reply, *we will, mother.*

"Thank you, daughters. I will miss you this evening, but you will not be missing from my heart."

"Thank you, mother. It is our pleasure to make these honorable sacrifices for you and our sisters." Mel adds, and Kari rolls her eyes knowing the little twat is just placating their mother.

As her two sisters make their way from the chamber, Kari can't decide where to move. Suddenly, it's her name that she hears bouncing off the rock, through the chamber entrance.

"Kari. Come in here please."

That alien anxiety creeps back over her, and Kari knows she must obey. She gathers her feet and moves to the chamber, passing Mel and Willow along the way. Mel lingers as they pass one another, making sure that Kari can see the pompous sneer across her face. Oh how Kari would love to throw the little maggot against a wall another time or two, but that will have to wait.

Kari senses hostility the moment she crosses the threshold.

"Oh, sweet Kari. You must remember that curiosity killed the cat."

Deja Vu strikes Kari once more.

INSIDE THE BUDGET hotel room where the Kalischs are *actually* staying, Velvet arrives just in time to see them hatch along with their eight additional siblings. Making a total of ten emergents and Sierra, who would need to be re-woken with another kiss.

Dezi, Willow, Legends, and several more of her hatchlings are here. As Velvet closes the door behind her, she feels all eyes fall on her back. Once she's done all the locks, Velvet hops with fluttering ease atop the dinette table. Her eyes flip into their sapphire hives. Euphoria bursts throughout her senses as she looks down at them all.

Quickly, she tells the group to sit, and in near-unison, every head in the room plops downward before settling without a second thought.

This, she will never cease to enjoy.

1 2

PAUSE

Dak's frustration consumes him. He knows that Dexter had to be innocent of the Kalisch abduction because he had been out of the state coaching a basketball tourney when the girl had disappeared.

Paradiso had not seen the calendar when the pair had gone to investigate Dexter's home. So, the alibi only lives with Dak for now, and he finds pause to come forward with it.

The heroes have been on a PR tour, taking part in multiple press conferences these past few days, and undermining all of that might cost him not only his career but possibly the truth.

Besides, yesterday's press conference had been the most eventful yet.

There's a singular moment in particular, at the very end of the presser. It doesn't even last a second, more like a single frame. But, Dak has watched it to the point of insanity. He's *this close* to pulling in an expert from forensics to get him the still image he needs, but Dak's hesitant to draw anyone else into this madness.

The one person he truly needs — Ghini Freeman — has

seemingly dropped off the face of the Earth. Dak has not heard from her once since she and Clemens left town. They should have been home several days ago, and Dak is beyond worried that not only has she not returned, but he hasn't been able to get ahold of her or her traveling companion either.

As the first lights of dawn begin to sneak over the horizon, Dak decides to go to the bench for a cigarette. Haunted by this obsession, Dak brings his tablet with him. He has to be able to continue comparing the images and definitively determine whether or not they are connected.

With the first hit of nicotine sliding through his veins, Dak taps the screen and pulls up the picture of Ghini's doppel-gänger from all those months ago.

He so desperately wants to delete the image for good and smash anything that might have a copy. It had not been something he had noticed at first. Only after Ghini pointed it out, did he take note of the woman's unsettling eyes. And now he can't unsee them, as the image grows more vivid and unnerving in his mind. It is without a doubt his worst night-mare to have to look at this over and over again. It's practi-cally a form of self-mutilation.

'What's wrong with her eyes?' Ghini's voice echoes inside him.

It had unsettled him then. But now, he's traumatized by the image of Paradiso's stupid moth living fresh atop his memories.

It takes all Dak's willpower to fight the phobic urge to abandon the tablet. There is nothing more paramount at this moment for him, than to investigate the blurry image further. At first, he'd wanted to write it off as a trick of the lens. However, that was a theory he was never fully convinced explained away the photo. The alternative explanation wasn't quite something he'd been conditioned to believe.

Dak's gaze traverses across the doppelgänger's face once again, which only serves to fluster him more than he already is. He needs a brief reprieve to focus on his nicotine fix as he swipes the image away and returns to that most recent press conference.

He grabs the little slider on the video player's timeline and drags just shy of the end. This is the only part he needs to see for the umpteen-trillionth time.

" . . . and this is Queenie Jeffords for —"

Damnit.

Dak needs to pause it just right, but he continues to fail.

Just like with the doppelgänger's image, Dak wants to chalk this one up to a trick of the lens, but the more he watches, the more he becomes convinced this is no optical illusion. He had seen the flicker across Detective Bradley's eyes when the reporter did her sign-off the first time he had watched the presser live.

It was certainly something odd, yet strangely, he had not been concerned, well at first. It was only later on that he found himself fixating on that brief flicker, and he continued to do so as more time passed. With each play, Dak grew plagued by a fear that he must prove could not be true. He needed the revelation that his mind was playing tricks on him.

Now, all these hours later, he's noted that the flicker of Bradley's eyes happens right after the reporter says her first name. *Queenie.* And by the time she's pronounced her surname, *Jeffords*, there's no disputing how ordinary Bradley's eyes are.

The moment is such a tiny sliver of a window that Dak feels incapable of utilizing the technology at his disposal effectively. Yet, even if he had someone skilled, like Legends, capable of operating the technology to its fullest potential,

Dak remains unsure that he could win the internal struggle of dissuading himself against this being something supernatural.

If he could, Dak would just call his granny and ask if one of her ghost stories matches these eyes. Unfortunately, the old bird's fallen down the rabbit hole of Alzheimer's and is likely incapable of any such conversation. Only a singular confirmation is needed. Someone to convince him that he isn't crazy.

Whatever's left, no matter how impossible. . .

He sighs and tries to play the video again. This time, he catches the still almost perfectly. Bradley can be seen over the reporter's shoulder, alas Dak's luck may not be that good. The camera only has the reporter in focus. The day-to-day details of Bradley's face are fuzzy, making her eyes almost imperceptible.

Dak is not a quitter though. He tries to pinch and zoom on a screenshot. *That,* he has managed to figure out how to do on his own. The pixels on the screen are as grainy as freshly harvested potatoes, the more he stretches the image. The quality of the video had not been the best to begin with. Still, Dak can distinctly make out that the eyes look off.

It could certainly be said that it was a trick of the lighting, or bad internet, or maybe an incompetent videographer, but, Dak knows the truth. Those eyes are the same ones as the grainy doppelgänger.

His mind's eye can picture them in clear detail sending his entire body into a ragged state of tension. Sweat beads up around the entirety of his hairline. Goosepimples line his flesh, and a weight on his chest feels like it's actively attempting to stifle his breathing. Every fiber of his anatomy begs Dak to look away. To run. To smash anything remotely resembling the image of those eyes.

He pulls a notepad from his jacket pocket and writes:

1) Doppelgänger
2) Car-Ee
3) 2nd Campsite Woman?
4) Bradley

He pauses for a brief second to consider one final name, which he ultimately writes down with conviction.

5) Legends?

13

THE BLACK HILLS GIANT

When the bus arrives in Rapid City, it's only a few minutes shy of midnight.

Ghini entertained the idea of returning to her apartment, but Samuel is rather convincing when it comes to his notion that they need to stick together for the night.

After the nightmares of the last week, the thought of being alone once night has fallen, creates a dreadful sense of terror for Ghini. She knows it should be the safest time of the day to avoid these creatures, but rational thinking went out the window the moment she accepted the reality of monsters — ones that could be walking right next to her on the street or standing behind her at the store without her knowing.

Samuel books a hotel room within walking distance of the bus station, and as they settle in for the night, he confirms they have a ride lined up for the morning. Despite their exhaustion, neither of them sleeps well.

Ghini dreams of claws, monsters, and *fire.*

The following morning, Ghini tries to shower. It has been over a week since she last stood beneath hot water. The normally soothing act is anything but. The heat reminds her of flames, and in a flustered panic, she foregoes the shower.

Trying to put that failure behind her, she dresses and heads down to the lobby where she's assaulted by stagnant humidity. She can feel the perspiration sticking to her within the seconds it takes to spot Samuel. He's sat in a frayed armchair, his face dotted with sweat.

A dusty vending machine is the only hope for a reprieve. Unfortunately, it spits out lukewarm bottles of water. At least, they will provide momentary relief from the stifling heat.

"Stay at my place." Samuel's voice sounds dry. "It'll be safer. We gotta know that neither of us has turned." Ghini passes him a water, and he takes a quick swig, "Into one of those — *things.*"

Those things.

The words resound through Ghini.

Jeannie could be one of 'Those things.'

Samuel is right though. It is not safe for either of them to move carelessly on their own. Making for an easy sale. She had not even considered the thought of Samuel turning and her not being able to trust him.

The hours begin to stretch as they sit waiting, sweating up a storm in the dingy lounge. "There he is," Samuel says as a dusty-brown, two-door, pickup-truck parks out front with an assortment of junk piled in the bed high above the cab.

Ghini is grateful for the comfort of a summer's breeze, even if the air outside is just as hot and muggy as it had been inside.

"Lumpy. Abandon us for some litter, eh?" Samuel says loudly over the puttering engine.

Lumpy's even more tanned than Samuel and could be two decades older for all she knows. His skin has the appearance of a weathered moleskin cover. A lemon-sized lump protrudes above his ear, and Ghini becomes mortified by the man's nickname.

"Sorry, Samuel. You know me, I had to." He articulates with the semi-slurred speech of someone hard of hearing, possibly deaf, before directing his gaze toward Ghini. "Lumpy's cuz a my last name, Lumpp. Two Ps. Get it? Lumpp." The man lets loose a giant's chortle as Samuel climbs into the cab, and she now notices the thin wire feeding from his ear.

"Sorry Mr. Lumpy, I just . . . I didn't expect you to be . . ." Her words are slow and deliberate as she makes the extra effort to emphasize the way her lips move. Yet, the act makes her feel as if she's doing something wrong, maybe even insensitive. His piercingly hazel eyes don't ease her anxiety.

"What, *disfigured*? Or *deaf*?" He laughs hysterically.

"Don't mind Lumpy, he's a comedian." Samuel beckons her toward the cab. "And possibly the greatest junk artist the Black Hills have ever known."

"Thanks Samuel!" Lumpy feigns a histrionic display of batting his eyelashes amid more laughter. "Garbage art is my passion."

Climbing into the cramped cab, Ghini notes it's tidier than she expected. She belts herself in next to Samuel, who is squished awkwardly on the hump of the bench seat between Lumpy and herself.

"I do write jokes though. And weld some damn good art. I just can't hear jack, 'cept this dull white noise unless I got my hear-ey aids in. And there's no shame in my little lump buddy neither." He laughs so heartily that Ghini almost thinks the joy makes him look a decade, if not two, younger.

"Do you mind if I ask —"

"*How I got these scars?*" He says with more fitful joy at his poor Heath Ledger impersonation, pointing to his — *'lump buddy.'*

"Lumpy . . ." Samuel glares.

"So we got No-Fun-Samuel in the car today. Oh well, I'm used to him. But, you wanna know how this all happened?" He asks waving a hand around his head. Highlighting the concerning mass beneath the skin.

"Got kicked in the head by a mule when I was nineteen. Trying to impress some cowgirls at the fair, and next thing I know, I wake up in the hospital. A week's gone by and people in lab coats and scrubs talk to me nonstop. But I couldn't hear a G-D thing. Terrifying it was.

"My hearing did come back a day or so later. Then it sounds like I'm underwater for couple'a weeks, but I think I'm all good. Then, right before my twenty-first birthday, I start noticing the hearing issues again, and I get this horrible pain behind my eyes. Turns out there's a tumor in there, benign, but it presses against my ear nerves. And I been steady losing my hearing since. Apparently, my old lump buddy is just a byproduct of the tumor and the trauma from being kicked in the head by a jackass."

His laughter is nearly akin to the *hee-haw* of a mule, and Ghini can't restrain her own giggles. Even Samuel seems more lighthearted, and he's been wearing his frustrated heart on his sleeve since they'd dealt with *Momma Montoya*.

THEY'D SPENT the entirety of that fateful day watching the Montoya's trailer burn and smolder a tempestuous black smoke into the air.

Despite the lingering darkness, neither the fire department nor the police ever came. Not even the smell of burnt marijuana coating the air brought about authorities or concerned neighbors.

Neither Ghini nor Samuel knew what to do. They had no way to put out the fire, and it felt unwise to turn their backs on the den of monsters. Instead, they opted to get as far away as possible without losing sight of the trailer.

Fear gripped both of them. At any moment a deadly hand could shoot through the debris.

Could *Momma* still be alive?

Then what would they do?

As the sky turned dark above the banner of shadowy smoke, the flames reached the gas tanks behind the trailer and ignited with a percussive explosion.

Still, no one came to investigate.

After the debris finished hailing down from deathly clouds above, their pistols became permanently fixed on the remnants of the building. If Momma or Lawson emerged from the chaos, they were ready.

Samuel noticed thunderclouds in the distance. With Ghini concentrated on the wreckage, he constructed a ramshackle shelter out of farming equipment, only finishing with the assistance of the light from the simmering flames. Unfortunately, it offered little protection from the elements, and neither of them slept.

When morning came, both were soaked to the bone. Only once the sun had drifted high above the prairie, did they venture out into the morning.

They cautiously surveyed the debris under a cloudless sky. There, Samuel found the remnants of three gas canisters. One propane, one a pesticide, and the last, the sleeping gas Manny had mentioned. Both of the latter two gases were heavily concentrated according to the charred information that survived.

Ghini hoped the sleeping gas had gotten to Manny in time. But, in her gut, she knew it likely had not.

What his death must have been like . . .

A tear trickled from her eye, and the floodgates opened as they trekked back toward Samuel's truck. Amidst tears, Ghini offered a silent prayer for Manny and his family. She prayed they would all reunite in heaven. Their penance being two decades of time served in a monstrous hell.

When they reached the end of the crops, the pair found Samuel's truck burnt to a crisp. The logical explanation was to blame Lawson. And things only got worse from there.

Samuel's phone had been in his glove box, which no longer existed beyond a mass of melted plastic and warped metal. Meanwhile, Ghini couldn't locate hers. She knew it must have slipped from her pocket during the skirmish in the subbasement. Unsure of what to do next, they surveyed the property.

Their luck seemingly turned when they uncovered an ATV hidden behind the brothers' living quarters. After locating the keys, they gathered what little they had left and set out for Flandreau proper. There, they'd find a phone, make a few calls, and find a ride back to Rapid City. Or so they hoped.

To their dismay, the ATV died less than halfway to Flandreau. The only option left had been to hoof it beneath the veil of a cloudless summer humidity.

Upon reaching the city limits, the sun was in its final quarter of the sky and night was fast approaching.

Luck had seemed to finally go their way when they got the last room at the first motel they visited. Unfortunately, another two days passed before they could leave Flandreau. Their first bus had been canceled due to maintenance. Another night in the ramshackle Motel awaited them as a rental car was practically unheard of in the area.

The bad luck piled up when the bus they finally managed

to get on, broke down halfway to Rapid City. They were comped a motel room for the night and given tickets for a bus the next day, which thankfully had no malfunctions, and delivered them to Rapid City without a hitch, albeit late that next evening.

AS LUMPY TURNS OFF the interstate for the roadways carving through the Black Hills, the truck feels lighthearted and jovial. Ghini could almost forget the horrors of this last week as Lumpy discusses his standup routine, opening for A-list stars, and selling his artwork. Somehow it also comes up that his name is Jeffrey, which does not suit him, in Ghini's opinion.

Here, in the heart of the hills, sprawling dark gray and black stones tower overhead, smattered with the gorgeous greens of the forest. But the serenity is short-lived.

"Did you two hear they found that missing girl?"

Ghini's ears perk up. She instantly thinks of Jeannie but hope deflates quickly.

It's not my baby.

"That old SDSU quarterback, Legends, I think, Johnathan Legends? Eh, don't sound right. But yeah he found that girl held captive by this huge goon. Man kept her locked up in his basement. Don't know what he did to her, but apparently, it weren't good if ya trust the grapevine.

"Guy killed a hostage too. That was before he shot the quarterback. But they put a bullet in the guy's head, so no need to worry about more missing girls. I betcha they're worried he might have had previous victims. Creeps me out. Specially cuz the guy was a giant. Like seven feet tall, *and,* works with kids. He's a teacher or a coach or something, can't remember, but how messed up is that?"

Ghini no longer listens. In all her years living in Rapid City, she only ever knew one man who fit that description. *What if she had stumbled upon a world of monsters only to learn that one of her closest friends was the real terror?*

"Do you remember the guy's name?" Her voice cracks.

Lumpy looks bewildered. "Sorry, the hearing aids don't work like most people think," he says trying to meet her gaze. "I hear muffled sounds that become easier to make out when I read lips."

Embarrassment heats her cheeks, and Ghini feels the need to retreat into herself. She hardly notices the changing scenery as he pulls into Deadwood.

Samuel's home sits atop a hill overlooking the town. After climbing the mountainous hillside, Lumpy enters a subdivision full of massive houses called, *Oak Hills*. The streets are lined with rows of oversized, well-manicured oak trees.

Deep within the neighborhood is a large brickwork monolith. A cement plaque near the top is embossed with shiny silver engraved letters that read, *Oak Acres*.

There appear to be fewer properties here, but all sit above the other subdivision. A menagerie of honest-to-God mansions. Houses with four double-car garages, yards bigger than Ghini's apartment complex, and more windows than she's ever seen before. And surprisingly, most are for sale.

"Those weren't there when I left," Samuel mutters.

"The for sale signs?" Samuel responds to Ghini's question with a grunt and a nod. "Wild. Looks like most have sold already." Ghini notes they all have the same realtor, Stephanie Fumero.

"Yeah. Odd, aint it? Maybe a developer trying to do something? Don't know."

Lumpy cracks a joke about developers and gold diggers

that Ghini doesn't quite understand, but Samuel chuckles, so she figures it must be good.

"Guess the neighbor kid stopped picking up the paper," Samuel says to no one in particular as the truck rattles its way into a long semi-circle drive, where a stack of newspapers on the front walkway has noticeably piled up.

The house looks like a ski resort. It's rustic and has lots of dark wood paneling and dark windowsills. There's not another building like it on the long winding street, but it suits Samuel. It's the most modest home amidst the limited drag of rivaling structures.

"You live here?" She asks disbelievingly.

"Since ninety-three."

Samuel nudges her back to reality so they can exit the car. Lumpy offers them each a handshake and is sure to let Ghini know what a pleasure it was to meet her. Just before they can shut the door, Lumpy asks that she get his number from Samuel in case she ever needs free tickets to a show.

They all wave goodbye and the rickety truck totters back down the road from whence it had come. Samuel turns and leads her up the footpath to the stoop when she notices a headline on one of the newspapers.

CHILDREN'S COACH RESPONSIBLE FOR MULTIPLE MISSING WOMEN

WITHOUT HESITATION, Ghini rips the paper from its plastic wrapping and unfurls it beneath her fingers, revealing two photos. One is Detective Legends and the missing white girl, both on gurneys giving thumbs-ups as they are wheeled into an ambulance. Then there's the picture that sinks her heart.

The caption breaks it.

Pictured here, Todd Dexter, local AAU basketball coach, was shot and pronounced dead on the scene during an altercation with RCPD detectives after killing one woman and kidnapping another. Locals have dubbed him The Black Hills Giant.

14

SUBJECTS

Everything from Velvet's life after Queenie feels like that Bill Murray movie. The one where he has to relive the same day over and over again.

Every memory from before feels like a dream.

Just like in the movie, the rigamarole of her life begins as soon as she wakes. She meets with Queenie, who explicitly outlines Velvet's daily tasks, including that she helps with the hatchlings before she is dismissed into the world with some other task like hunting for food or bringing home a swathe of new sisters. She has no problem doing either, but Velvet is without a doubt glad that she has gone on her last errand run from the cave. They will finally be able to move Queenie and the rest of her colony somewhere much safer and more secure.

It also means Velvet would not stay with Queenie this evening. Her mother expects her to complete all the final preparations for their new hive by the following morning. Thankfully, Velvet has been done with those preparations for several days now, which has given her the time necessary to invest in her own side project.

Now that she has taken in the lay of the land surrounding their new home, she returns up the hillside. A pang of hunger eats away at her gut the further into the day she goes. As if vocalizing her growling appetite, the squeaks and rumblings of a rickety vehicle shake nearby. An auditory intruder on an otherwise serene afternoon.

On instinct, Velvet flutters out of sight. She knows her appearance is memorable, and she refuses to leave anything up to chance. Once the old truck has wheeled far enough into the distance, Velvet finishes her trek, and decides to use the rear entrance to avoid being seen from the main roads.

Inside, the static from Legends' police scanner floods her hearing. A safety net she put in place on the off chance that the city's finest discover the colony's presence.

To her frustration, Velvet notices that not one of her children is there keeping tabs on the thing.

Children.

She scoffs at the idea.

Queenie dotes on her progeny.

Well, she had. Lately, however, that warmth and affection, the nicknames, the touches; they all seem — *colder*, more calculating. Her behavior has switched from earning respect to commanding it.

And still, the colony grows. Only now, there appears to be a strategic design that Velvet can't help but marvel at. Queenie has begun telling the daughters to acquire new members from specific areas and trades. They've coordinated their excursions at random intervals, ensuring that there's no semblance of a pattern developing.

Velvet on the other hand thinks of the hatchlings she's

fostered and in her mind, she considers them more — *subjects.* They serve her.

But there is something more than pure subjugation. These women are her research. Her experimental subjects.

She has always been clever, but life after assimilation bends to her will like a lucid dream. Everything comes to her with ease, and she grows wiser and stronger with each passing day.

But one subject's behavior has proven to be counterproductive to Velvet's needs moving forward.

Sierra.

She might be Velvet's first experiment, but the girl is also one of Queenie's. A fact that hasn't produced much as far as tangible insights, but she thinks that the girl's mind has gone through such heavy abuse, her inhibition has abandoned her. Velvet knew the girl was impulsive to begin with, but lately, she seems solely driven by the pleasure principle, and that feels dangerous.

No other subject has shown such a lack of tact or discretion. Then there's the girl's libido. She's caught the girl taking liberties with the drones, and according to Dezi, involving other sisters in her hedonistic activities.

It appears today is no different. The wails of a banshee perforate the monotony of the static blanketing the room. Velvet's jaw sets underneath a weighty rage. This girl is proving to be out of her control, so what use will she have for her moving forward?

None.

Sierra has served her purpose, but she has become cancerous to Velvet's plans, and unchecked, the girl may metastasize into other members of the colony and that is something Velvet can't have. Even if they can avoid that, Velvet worries the girl might betray her to Queenie and her eyes. No one can overcome their mother's gaze, not even Velvet. Somehow she can remain quite lucid during these affairs, but it doesn't matter as her body and mind betray her at Queenie's beck and call.

Maybe there is a willingness to give in though. Ever since Velvet had been assimilated into the colony, she has always yearned for her mother's attention. It's a chemical addiction. One she believes stems from pheromones. Whenever Queenie's scent is near, Velvet is mindful of the endorphins rushing through her. Even though she recognizes this, Velvet refuses to do anything about it.

Why?

Well, she has to admit, she enjoys the rush. Like a junkie.

A junkie — that's what Sierra has become.

As a teenager, Velvet struggled when they had to put her cat down, but during that dreadful affair, she learned how commonplace death was, and how often it rears its head each day. So, her outlook evolved.

Death took the weakest and the strongest. The healthiest and the despondent. There was no need to fear Death because everyone was judged equally in Death's eyes.

Her short legs stride with purpose as she enters the room. The soundtrack of pleasure doesn't deter Velvet, and she doesn't even pause to take in the strangeness of the acts playing out before her.

Instead, she grabs Sierra by the back of the head, her long nails sink into the crown of the girl's scalp. An ephemeral sensation halts the breath within Velvet's chest, giving her a brief pause to experience the transition of the tactile sensations to something more metaphysical.

In this moment, Velvet notices the presence of two more beings.

Sierra's parents.

The couple has been restrained with an excessive number of zip ties to the two dining chairs that they currently sit atop. Their eyes are peeled open with heavy-duty duct tape. And yet, neither look perturbed by what they see. They almost look peaceful. Even as Velvet flicks their limp rag doll of a daughter from her fingertips, purposefully landing the corpse at their feet, their expressions remain tranquil.

The sight is pathetic. The entire family is about as valuable as bodily waste.

Velvet had seen the videos of them on TV. Sierra had shared stories too. These were not valuable assets.

With her mind made up, Velvet quickly closes the distance between herself and the captives. Her fingers slash with such ferocity that the depths of her cuticles penetrate each of their throats in one long sweeping motion, leaving them wide open like a gaping mouth.

Now all that remains is Detective Legends. Velvet considers removing him from play as well, but decides to leave him right where he is. She might need him after all. "Legends, you're done for the night. Wake up at sunrise."

"Of course, Velvet."

As she leaves the room, locking the door from the outside, she lets loose a devilish snicker, believing that the entire world seems to be spinning her way.

15

SCHEMES

That first day, when Mel had been reborn, the wheels inside her head began turning differently.

The first chance she got, she began to test herself. Queenie would send her out to hunt and forage, but from the outset, that was never her priority. She devoted herself to learning her surroundings and mastering her new self. She had only lived in the area a few weeks with her mother when they'd been taken, so most of the area still remained novel to her.

It became clear that Rapid City would be her best hunting ground. It was close, with tiny little pockets of communities. All of which naturally segments from one another. But the more she explored the terrain, the more she grew curious about her new state of being and the woman who had bestowed it upon her. Hence, her trips to the Rapid City Public Library. There, she learned of a missing girl, Jeannie Freeman, who disappeared over six months ago. Much too young to be Queenie, or so she initially thought. Except, there was a picture of the girl's mother. *Ghini Freeman*. A strange name to say the least, but she was the spitting image of Queenie, maybe add ten years.

As it turns out, Ghini had been a reality TV star when she was younger, and those photos were the spitting image of Queenie.

So, Mel came back to the library, did her research, and exhausted any leads she could find. But the more she watched the assimilation process unfold for her and her sisters, the more her theory took root.

She'd tried to locate more family, ruling out other possibilities. But there's no sister, no cousin, no aunt, niece, nephew, nothing. And as far as the public record is concerned, there certainly isn't any history of there ever being a *Queenie Freeman* in the area.

Just as a certain scheme began to consume Mel, Ghini strolled into the library, making a direct beeline for the computer banks below where Mel sat on the terrace above. She only needed to scoot a few seats down to have the perfect view of Ghini's computer. The woman was persistent. And an addict; hooked on her pills and voracious browsing of insects. More specifically, their eyes.

So she knows, Mel remembers thinking to herself.

There was no way it could be a coincidence, but Mel needed more. Her hunch felt supported, except she remained unsure of how to validate it entirely.

That is until Melissa Fumero made her move. From above, it was easy to survey the actions of many, and toward the end of Ghini's visit, she watched as Ms. Fumero offered a twenty-dollar bill to a young black girl. The girl then covertly maneuvered over to Ghini's computer when she'd gotten up for a coffee. The girl left a slip of paper on the keyboard and typed in a search that pulled up pictures of insects who had the same eyes as Mel herself. The hive eyes.

Unfortunately, Mel hadn't been quick enough to make a move on Fumero, but the young girl had lingered.

Dezi, Mel's true firstborn.

Still, she needed the Fumero woman. It was all too apparent that she knew things that Mel was surprisingly desperate to learn. Thankfully, Lady Luck had decided to take Mel's side.

As she left with her little Dezi in tow, Mel came across a stack of business cards for *Melissa Fumero Realty.*

The very next morning she had Fumero in her grasp.

Regrettably, Mel and Sierra's experiments on the woman seemed to break her down into nothing more than a mindless husk. Still, that husk had clout and served as a card up Mel's sleeve.

Before it had gotten too bad, Sierra and Mel were able to extract a trove of information regarding their own existence, while interrogating Fumero. Enough to try and reach out to Ghini and find a connection to Queenie. Even though Sierra had ad-libbed much of her conversation with Ghini, Mel felt the interaction had ultimately set the stage to lure the woman out into the open.

With an insatiable lust for power over Queenie beginning to dominate Mel's thinking, she devoted everything to controlling the one being who might have some sort of ability to manipulate Queenie.

THEN CAME the fateful moment when they set out to take Ghini.

Sierra makes the call as "Kay" to set up a face-to-face. Only, that had not been possible. Ghini was leaving town on some sort of fact-finding mission. One that, if successful, would shed more light on Velvet and her sisters' true nature. So, she decided to wait. Patience is something she has time for.

But the most important piece of this call had been a single word.

Likkle.

The same word that Queenie often used. Neither Dezi nor Sierra had ever heard anyone else use such a word. This felt like Velvet's vindication.

Ghini had said she'd be home in two days. But to Velvet's misfortune, two days go by, then three, then four, and they don't hear from her. Multiple attempts to get ahold of Ghini prove fruitless in the following days, and with a cynical certainty, Velvets presumes the woman has met an untimely demise.

She hopes it was at the hands of one of their kind.

Over a week passes and this fatalistic outlook appears more and more plausible. Each time they try her, the woman's cell goes straight to voicemail. Velvet takes this to mean that the device must either be off or dead, and may confirm her gut feeling regarding the woman's current state of being.

Still, Velvet thought of herself as pragmatic, and just to be sure, she had even commanded several of her children to stake out the woman's entire apartment complex. In all that time, not a single daughter or sister sees hide nor hair of the missing woman.

Then came golden boy Detective Legends with the intel that they so desperately needed. The likely identity of Ghini's travel companion — Samuel Clemens. A name that Velvet wouldn't easily forget.

When they made their move on his property they learned from a neighbor boy, who was quick to spill the beans, that

Mr. Clemens had yet to return to town despite it being nearly a week since he had departed.

While they couldn't get to Clemens or Ghini, Velvet's experiments led to a brand new discovery. The ease with which children's minds can be molded. The boy watching Clemens' house was no more than ten years old, but he followed directions with little effort from Velvet's hive eyes, and he opened many more doors for her.

Then one day as if from the blue, came the picture from the neighbor boy. Clemens was home, and he'd brought Ghini with him.

Now comes the final piece of her plan, and for this, Velvet has been gifted a versatile piece on the board.

Kari.

Velvet knows that Queenie's firstborn must have stumbled upon something that their mother did not want her to know. What that something is, she cannot say for certain.

Velvet has seen the signs with Sierra. She knows both herself and Queenie have separately toyed with the girl's mind. Their ability to erase and alter memories has clearly had far-reaching consequences that Velvet had not foreseen.

However, Queenie seems to have found much more regular use for it, specifically with Kari, for whatever reason.

When abused, Velvet is now aware of the ramifications. The sisters grow slower and are incredibly pliable, yet they also tend to be less inhibited. Which as it turns out is a combination that Velvet has recently discovered makes her sister more susceptible to Velvet's influences.

"I need you to go pay a visit to a friend tomorrow. You'll catch the bus to this dive of a cowboy bar in Deadwood called,

The Watering Hole. Make sure this woman isn't there." She pulls up a picture on what had been Sierra's cellphone. The vacant expression on her sister's face never changes as she nods her understanding.

"Excellent sister. Excellent." Velvet plants a nectar-filled kiss on her sister's plump lips, knowing that her influence will flood the girl in time.

16

THE WATERING HOLE

Samuel and Ghini spent the previous evening feeling unsettled in its normality.

Ghini had been brought to tears learning about what happened to Todd. It had to be a mistake, he would never hurt a fly. But what could she do? Dak's protege had shot her friend dead, and after all the craziness of the past few days, this was the final crack in her dam, and exhaustion poured through her.

Between the monotony of the evening and her bottomless melancholy, her existence feels hollow. That of a prisoner.

Sleep eventually came for her before she could ever leave Samuel's sectional. And when she finally awoke this morning, she was surprised at how refreshed she feels. Without a doubt the best sleep she's had in weeks. A dreamless slumber that ticked off the hours with the mere snap of the fingers.

So far, the morning is slow and uneventful. As Ghini makes her way down the stairs to join Samuel for breakfast, his voice rings out across the large open spaces of the home. "Calling an audible."

"Why? What's happened?" She feels her mind catapult into the catastrophes that might have occurred. A black smoldering cloud lifts into her reveries, and that's all she can see. An empty void, filled with silent screams, permeate her thoughts. She does her best to tune them out.

"Nothing to do with our infestation problem. Just got a call from Patty."

Patty Armstrong, Samuel's co-owner at *The Watering Hole* and its General Manager.

"Something's sprung a leak over at The Hole. Patty wants to call a plumber, but I ain't paying plumber's wages."

Ghini considers staying behind, avoiding the temptation of the bar, but she decides otherwise. "Then we go to Dak?" That had been the plan after all, and she can relent to detouring from it.

There is plenty of daylight left, but a twinge of anxiety palpitates in her chest. The thought of altering the day's agenda, she can deal with. But running into the man who killed her friend haunts her future, and she worries — well aware of the improbability of the situation unfolding at The WH — that Dak's former partner will be there lying in wait.

"Then we go to Dak," he confirms.

They eat a quick bowl of cereal each, and Ghini has only one cup of coffee, compared to Samuel's three, before they hurry out the door. As Samuel winds his truck through the quiet streets that direct them from the neighborhood, Ghini asks Samuel about his neighbors. She imagines all the big wigs from the surrounding hills owning these lavish hideaways.

"Next door's the local weatherman. Two down's the guy who invented the liquid bandaid. Sold the patent to the military. Across the street's a landowner. Two doctors in the next two houses. You get the picture."

"Geez Samuel, how the hell'd *you* end up here?" She asks,

considering the grand portion of the subdivision left in the rearview mirror.

"Been smart with my money. Plus, I been alive a long time."

"Clearly," she laughs out loud. The genuineness of it catalyzes a gentle warmth inside her.

Samuel exits the subdivision onto a backroad that winds through forested rocky hills until the scenery unfolds into the civilization of Deadwood's main road.

"Drop me off here?" Ghini asks pointing to a refurbished convenience store situated on the corner of the last intersection before the road dead-ends a quarter mile down at The WH.

"Sure. What d'ya need?"

"Something to drink that isn't alcohol."

"You know I got other things besides liquor and beer . . ."

"I know Samuel, I just . . . I'm kinda jonesing for a soda and some — some nicotine."

"The 'tine ain't easy to quit. Get you some pouches, not dip, the nicotine pouches. Couple bar flies been saying they help." He offers her a twenty, but she holds up a hand in protest as he pulls into the near-empty parking lot.

"Sure thing. Want anything?"

"Nope. Sure you can walk?"

"Samuel it's like a five-minute walk. I do it every time the bus drops me off right there." She points to the bus stop where a quartet of morning commuters sits waiting.

"That you do. See ya in ten?"

"Ouch. I don't walk that slow." She snickers closing the door behind her. This truck is for the construction company that Samuel moonlights at. A big white F-250 with all the bells and whistles.

Inside, Ghini grabs a sports drink, something off-brand, but it saves her almost two dollars. At the register, she foregoes the nicotine pouches for a disposable vaporizer. She can't remember the last time she'd had a fix, but she wants one now. She's been good. She's avoided booze, her stimulants, and all other vices, but she needs something to settle her nerves.

Yet, the normality of everyday reality is getting to her. Her purpose has become investigating monsters; without that, life feels too unsettling.

Blue skies are spotted like a leopard with the smallest fragments of clouds meandering above. A gentle breeze breaks up the stagnant humidity building as she leaves the comforting hum of the store's AC for the peace of the outside world.

She presses the vaporizer to her lips, tasting the sweet blueberry flavor that hits her with a cascading nicotine rush. The sensation waterfalls from her mind to her toes. Carrying with it an invisible weight she'd grown accustomed to lugging around.

Ghini takes a few more puffs along the walk and when she reaches the rustic bar, she sees the banged-up Toyota Carola belonging to Patty. But when she looks inside, there is no sign of Patty. The windows are a bit dusty, with some condensation forming within the panes, so Ghini moves down a window, away from the front entrance.

This window hasn't been compromised by condensation half as bad as its neighbor. As she peers through the double pane glass, she finds a view of the bar, where a tall blonde woman looms over the bartop with her back to Ghini. It looks like she's trying to get someone's attention, but as far as Ghini can tell, there isn't a single person inside except the blonde.

Suddenly, Samuel's head pops up several feet down from the woman, the long oaken slab conceals the majority of his figure. His expression reminds her of a prairie dog surveying a disturbance. A strange look overtakes his face. He goes from curious to placid.

Fear erupts inside Ghini. She's been too close to this. It could be a trigger from Flandreau. Regardless, she listens to the adrenaline telling her to move.

The vaporizer slips unnoticed from her hand as her gazelle-like strides bound her to the front door. She flings it open with more strength than she realizes and is inside before the old wooden door slams into the side of the building.

The blonde woman's attention swivels from Samuel to Ghini.

Ghini's first thought is about how pretty she thinks the woman looks.

Her second is a myriad of curses and swears as she glimpses the woman's eyes.

Quickly, she averts her gaze, and fortunately finds a fire extinguisher hanging on the wall beside her. She grabs the large red container and unhooks the nozzle. Instincts fire through her as she pulls the fire alarm next to the extinguisher housing.

Sprinklers begin pouring gushes of water from above. At first, the spray is warm and stale, but swiftly the downpour turns cold. The torrent makes it difficult for Ghini to see, but that will not stop her from charging the woman, who in return holds her ground, apparently curious of the situation unfurling.

Ghini flips the pin and just as she begins to spray the extinguisher's contents, she takes a deep hit to the collarbone and feels herself fly backward. The fire extinguisher's spray seems to add to her catapult-like launch, but it also connects directly with the monstrous woman.

She was quick. *Too quick*, Ghini thinks. Yet she refuses to stop spraying. The blonde yelps out like a dog that's just had its tail stepped on.

As she lands, Ghini slides across the slick hardwood. The

other woman stands nearly motionless beneath the torrential spray, foam washing off her. Despite having the wind knocked from her lungs, Ghini hastily gets back to her feet. Though, she is regretting the vaporizer now. Her breathing feels haggard. As if the vapor has already begun to stifle the muscles of her lungs.

As she charges the stranger, the woman turns and flees for the side door, stumbling like a drunk. She's fast, but nowhere near as quick as a moment ago. The door flies open, and Ghini's extinguisher puffs its last breath of foam as the woman tumbles into the sunshine.

Ghini feels the need for a firearm. She's certain that Samuel keeps a shotgun behind the bar like an old western saloon. She pulls herself over the bartop and flops to the other side. Beneath the well, she finds a double-barrel shotgun. She opens it, sees that it is not loaded, and scrambles to find the shells. It only takes a few seconds, but she worries the woman has gotten too far ahead of her.

Ghini sprints from behind the bar toward the exit, which opens up onto a view of the forest. There, she sees the blonde woman staggering and de-clothing in the distance. She flops onto a large rock in nothing but her birthday suit, and Ghini notes how skinny the woman is. Her ribs show beneath her breasts, and her hip bones protrude at sharp angles beneath her waistline.

Ghini lets loose a war cry and fires the double barrel once, but her target is too far away. She charges faster, stumbling and squeaking in her wet clothes, managing to fire off another shot as the naked woman flops from her sun-bathing rock.

A cry of pain shocks Ghini's senses as the woman staggers to her feet and sprints for the wilderness with the intensity of cornered prey. Ghini gives up pursuit upon reaching the stone and seeing the pool of blood that gathers at the foot of the bolder, before trailing off into the woods. A Rorschach of trickled droplets speaks to the path that the woman had taken in her hasty escape.

Then it dawns on her.

Where's Samuel?

She sprints back to the bar, where she splashes through giant puddles. The sprinklers have run out of fluid, and within the cool damp quiet of the saloon, there does not seem to be a single trace of Samuel anywhere.

Ghini has never felt more alone than she does right now.

17

CHANGING

As Queenie sits pondering the days to come and all that they will bring, a thought flickers through her mind. Already, her routine is a victim of change. And she does not care for it.

Her colony has grown so large, yet she knows them all. But now, there are variables. She thought Mel had been a controlled variable; unfortunately, Queenie gets the sense that she underestimated the girl.

She dares admit such shortcomings only to the thoughts in her head. Yet, it fails to diminish the pride she holds for her sweet Mel. The girl's craftiness and resiliency are to be admired, but her defiance and independence were things that needed to be nipped. It was only a matter of time before the girl learned the truth of her condition, and if Queenie doesn't have a plan, all that she built could be lost.

Then comes Kari. Another variable she believed was well under her control. However, her firstborn has thrown off Queenie's entire schedule for this evening. That is something

Queenie knows on instinct. Her internal clock has become the law of the land for the colony.

Now, for the first time ever, one of her children is not on schedule with Queenie's wishes, and still, she struggles excepting that the culprit is her precious Kari.

As the minutes drone on, a fury begins to well up inside of her. An internal voice stirs a potent discontent for the girl and her insolence this evening.

A conscious piece of her is quick to remind Queenie that this all may be her fault. The things she has done to Kari's memory may be to blame. But other thoughts drown that one in their cacophonous chorus. They instill in her the idea that Kari's mind must be weak. A stronger daughter would not be so crippled by Queenie's abilities.

Now her hunger is getting the best of her. It is fueling her rage, and she knows she will erupt soon if she does not get something to eat.

Then again . . . she has her meal, sat in the corner, head lolled to the side, vacant stare and pale complexion. Queenie knows Mel will not miss the woman, the contempt she has for her is clear by the scars across the woman's face. In the mass shuffle of things, she remains certain most would forget the useless daughter ever existed, like all the others before her.

A commotion overhead stirs her from the void of thoughts and voices that she contends with.

Queenie sees no need to be bothered by such disturbances. Yet, as the voices grow closer, so too do the footsteps that belong to each voice. One is laboring. A heavy footfall, followed by a slide.

Thump. Slide. Thump. Slide.

Although her peace and quiet are disturbed, her fury manages to subside. That splendid odor her firstborn gives off quiets her mind with reveries of that moment when she had looked upon Kari for the first time as a daughter. As the footfalls near, she notices a sourness to the scent. Something metallic. That's when the footsteps forego the ceiling above and can be felt reverberating down the stairs into the concrete floor beneath her feet.

A few seconds pass and at the bottom of the steps, her sweet Kari appears. A strange pang of worry bites through Queenie as she takes in her daughter's condition.

She has been shot. Her naked body is haggard and pale. Debris, dirt, and blood cake themselves across her daughter's smooth skin. Blood stains her chin, and her eyes uncontrollably pulsate with wild abandon.

"Mother," Kari croaks the word before crumbling like an avalanche to her knees.

The girl doesn't have an ounce of quit in her. The sight of her firstborn crawling across the dusty floor, with the deadweight of her legs dragging behind her, reminds Queenie of a seal. The useless appendages leave a streak of clean floor as she pulls herself through the dust toward her mother.

A tinge of concern is replaced with intrigue as she realizes that the girl's injuries appear non-life-threatening.

With her concerns abating, she feels the need to interrogate the girl. "What has happened to you, precious?"

"Is he here?"

"Tell me what happened, Kari."

In a daze her daughter mutters through chattering teeth, "There's a man in town. He's supposed to have picture-perfect memory." She lets out a wet cough. "I thought a man like that might be a piece on the board that we couldn't ignore."

Queenie's eyes press into slits as she warily asks, "You found this man?"

"Yes."

"What happened when you found him?"

"I was attacked."

This gives Queenie pause. *Attacked.* An odd choice of word. "Go on." She says as the girl's eyes lock onto her own.

"Someone came into the bar, behind me. They turned sprinklers on, they used a fire extinguisher. Then they shot me. I was so cold. I am *still* so cold."

The flat responses please Queenie. "Thank you, Kari, you will be warm soon, my firstborn." She feels a bright motherly smile crawl across her face as she thinks about the new roles she must provide her firstborn.

18

SURVEILLANCE

Dak spent over two hours in the car, simply driving. Then came the long droll of hours engulfed in the stagnant heat consuming his sedan as darkness overwhelmed the sky. While his efforts seem to have paid dividends, it's not quite clear to Dak what that evidence truly speaks to — well, other than the *homicide* . . .

Regardless, he is grateful for the gut instinct that took him there.

Earlier that afternoon, Dak had arrived for his night shift and everything felt normal. But as he settled in, and his daytime counterparts left, something ate away at Dak.

Legends' flat affect carried him all the way out the door. A split-second decision got Dak on his feet. He has simply had enough of this odd behavior. There's no desire to be caught snooping on his ex-protege, so he quickly devises a believable yarn about tying up some loose ends with the Kalisch kidnapping investigation. Hopefully, that'd be enough to cover his ass with The Chief and God forbid, Legends, should it come down to that.

It was a slow and arduous drive all the way out to Legends' home in the hills surrounding Deadwood. One of those days when all the rams and elk had decided it was their turn to use the roadways, delaying the flow of traffic.

Then there were the tourists, forever traversing the hills' many twists and curves at sluggish intervals.

When he finally arrives in Deadwood, Dak makes sure to watch from afar, gambling on the fact that the kid wouldn't recognize his vehicle. Even if his old beater sticks out like a sore thumb in this particular neighborhood.

Kid had to have gotten paid in college, but good for him.

The thought bred a burst of laughter amidst the stagnant humidity of the car.

Now, that laughter feels so far away. Like it had belonged to a dream, it never existed. In the present, Dak feels nothing but anger and pity.

He'd just left the kid.

Sat there.

In that room with the corpses of all three Kalisch family members.

The difficulty with which Dak had to endure the sight of the girl using Legends as a meat doll was unimaginable. Although, watching her zip-tie her parents to a couple of chairs, forcing them to spectate, was an uncomfortably close second. The parents looked like they were on something, some sort of drug that kept them perfectly still.

But what frightened Dak to his core . . .

Why his hands ache from the death grip he had kept on the camera . . .

Why they shake throughout the entirety of his drive home . . .

And, why he couldn't bring himself to make an arrest despite his overwhelming evidence . . .

The buzzcut girl.

She clearly had red hair. She wasn't large or anything, but even from his distant vantage point, Dak could feel the emanation of sinister intentions.

The girl's back blocked his view, and he couldn't see how she'd killed the Kalisch girl. But he had gotten a clear photo of Buzzcut tossing the youngest Kalisch like a rag doll. Such strength seemed inhumanly possible, especially considering the girl's size.

He couldn't see the Kalisch girl's body on the ground, but he had gotten a photo of Buzzcut taking out the parents as well. It had been quick, and Dak couldn't be certain what blade was used. It must have been something small and easily concealable. Whatever it was, it'd been sharp and efficient at taking out both parents with ease.

There had only been a single good chance to capture Buzzcut's face on camera. When she had gone to leave the room, she turned her head, just enough. It'd only been a photo in profile, but it was enough to capture the girl's features.

Throughout the entirety of this ordeal, Dak took note that Legends never moved. As he reviews the photos from the safety of his desk, Dak thinks of a Ken doll sitting up against the headboard. The kid looks broken, hardly alive. All that youth and charisma and naiveté vanished entirely. Like the kid was dead, and his body moved onward without a soul.

The night drags its feet like a petulant child and Dak needs some coffee if he's going to be able to force himself through the remainder of the shift.

Unfortunately, he needs some privacy, which is hard to come by at the precinct. Especially when officers regularly came to Dak for advice.

Thankfully, Paradiso had microwaved some fried catfish

that stank up the break room enough that no one even dare enter the stench's far-reaching orbit.

Situated in the privacy of the room, Dak pours himself a cup of coffee and drops a couple of ice cubes in, to water down the delinquent taste. Coffee in hand, he clicks through the last flurry of photos and finds that moment when Buzzcut turns her head, and that's when he sees it.

The photo is dark, but he's certain he sees them.

He drops the file into his photo editor and flips the brightness and the vibrance. There, clear as day, are two sapphire-blue moth's eyes filling the girl's pale face. Dak slams the laptop shut and lights a cigarette then and there, unsure of what to say once someone reprimands him for smoking indoors — though, he is likely to find a way that he can blame it on the fish.

19

HELP

The construction company truck that Samuel had driven them in, is weighty beneath Ghini's hands, but it's nothing she can't handle thanks to the adrenaline still coursing through her.

Instantly, she had made the decision for what her next course of action need be. It was a duty she felt she owed, but, more importantly, it was the most logical move.

Although, it is not until Ghini has left the hills in her rearview and is looking down into Rapid City that the gravity of what she is doing finally settles. Without a single shred of doubt encircling her actions, a burning conviction weighs down the accelerator beneath her foot.

She gasses the truck along steep winding hills and blows through the outskirts of town, beelining her way East. It's tough going trying to find the tiny little town without GPS or a phone, but Samuel has an atlas in the truck and after she pulls off on the side of the highway, she gets her bearings. With little to no trouble, she finds her way back to the gravel road leading into the tiny village of Interior.

She pulls up outside the church where she had met Bernie all those weeks ago, but the doors are locked and the beer boxes covering up the windows have been replaced with pristine panes of glass and new trim. Capable of peering through the immaculate apertures, she can see that the Church itself is empty.

She has no idea where to go next. She is half tempted to start knocking on doors, but then she thinks about it and decides that if Bernie is anything like his uncle, Ghini feels confident assuming where he will be.

The town is so small it doesn't take much time for Ghini to wheel the truck up to a sliding halt across the gravel parking lot of the tiny brown-paneled tavern.

Inside, she is hit with a tinge of nostalgia and sadness as she sees Bernie. His shaggy hair held back with a bandana, arms pinned out against the bar, talking to patrons just like Samuel would.

The kid notices her almost as soon as she's through the door. He doesn't appear thrilled at her sudden appearance and raises an eyebrow in confusion. Yet, concern lingers at the tail of his glance.

Bernie upends himself from the bar and gestures for her to move toward an exit near the back. He gets there first and nods to an older woman talking to a table of grizzled-looking laborers. Her frizzy greyed hair bobs as the woman returns the motion. She quickly finishes up with her patrons and heads toward the bar, likely to assume Bernie's position during his absence.

That taken care of, he holds the door for Ghini and follows her out into the afternoon heat. When she turns around to address Bernie, he's already got a cigarette lit between his lips.

"You know those things are bad for you?" Ghini hears the

words that had been directed toward her so many times, echo between her ears.

"I'm aware."

The lull between them leaves Ghini uncomfortable. She has no clue where to go from here. Her initial thought is to make small talk, which she regrets almost instantly. "So, you're a bartender too? Jack of all trades, like your uncle, eh?"

"Yup. Got a stake in the place too."

Just like Samuel. Short and to the point. She could take a lesson from that, but her thoughts flounder as she sputters through the interaction. "Just like your uncle. I'm surprised how much you do for the community here. I drove by the Church. It looks good."

"'Preciate it. Just doing good by the community that took me in. They're good people here." He pauses and before Ghini can decide what to say next, Bernie chimes in with surprising purpose in his voice. "Around here, labels don't mean too much outside of '*Interiorite*' or not. If you help the town and be kind to your neighbor most people don't think much about ya. That don't mean I haven't had my fair share of problems now and then, but they're good people here."

"Good. I'm glad." She feels a flush of pride on her face. A maternal instinct. The same she would have for her own daughter when Jeannic came home with her growing insights and morals that demonstrated her growth into a young woman of high character.

"But you've got bad news. Don't you?" He says inhaling deeply on the elongated nicotine death stick.

"I — how'd you know?"

"Why else are you, and *only you,* here?" He inhales once more against the dwindling tobacco and croaks out, "What other explanation is there? Especially if you didn't call."

He is without a doubt, right. She cannot think of another

feasible explanation, so there's no reason to beat around the bush. She might as well tell him everything.

"Did Samuel ever talk to you about a man named Manny Montoya?" Bernie shakes his head while the ember at the end of his cigarette flares. "Well, he — Montoya — had *one*. One of those creatures. Locked up in a bunker. He called it a *Vespid*, and . . ." she trails off deciding to omit the specifics of how that encounter played out.

Bernie doesn't say a thing. The only sound between them is the subtle crackle of his cigarette as it consumes itself.

"But we got back to town, and Samuel had to go by the bar. He dropped me off down the street at a convenience store, but when I got to The WH there was a woman there. She was one of them. She'd hypnotized Samuel. She was so fast. I got her with Samuel's shotgun after slowing her down with a fire extinguisher, but she got away." The next words catch in her throat, still she manages to force them out. "And Samuel's missing."

It's that last bit where Bernie perks up and the emotions rooted in what Ghini has just said break his calm facade. "What do you mean he's *missing*?" The crestfallen look consumes his eyes and though it doesn't look like he will cry, there is a vivid pain behind them.

"I think *they* have him. I lost him amidst the craziness with that *thing*. Then I drove straight here. I think —"

"Okay. I'm in." He cuts her off with a blazing look of determination across his brow.

"In what?"

"You want my help, right?"

Ghini hadn't quite thought about that as far as an ask. She had predicted that Bernie could provide more knowledge and theories, but she had not anticipated dragging him back into this nightmare.

Only now, does she realize how alone she is. More than ever, a desire to bolster her pack sounds like a good idea. The odds weren't in her favor as a lone wolf, and she finally accepts that she could use all the allies she can get.

A terrifying memory loops its traumatic words through her mind.

Twenty years.

She can't let Samuel become one of those things for twenty years, not over her dead body.

"Alright. Pack your stuff then. We've got to get back to RC and pay a little visit to a friend of mine. We're going to need *a lot* of help."

20

ORDERS

Velvet enjoys the fact that she doesn't have to share a space with Queenie. The autonomy of their new dynamic is liberating.

Despite needing to make the occasional stop by her mother's, Velvet's days have become mostly her own. She is in charge of herself and several sisters, not to mention her own daughters. But come day's end, she must always report to Queenie.

Now, as nightfall crests on another day, Velvet has arrived at her mother's to touch base. But she's shocked to find a sickly-looking Kari guarding the stairwell that leads down to their mother's private sanctum. This is the first time in several days that she has seen her sister. The last time she had been around Kari, Velvet had been giving her the order to abduct her new favorite drone, Clemmy.

She is well aware that Kari accomplished her goal, but she does not know why the woman looks so haggard and out of sorts. There aren't any signs of visible injuries, but her skin tone is pale and tinted with an unsightly hue.

"What happened to you?"

The girl's eyes are lifeless. Yet, they roll downward to meet Velvet's at the sound of her voice. "What do you need?"

Velvet isn't put off by the question, but the lack of acknowledgment for her inquiry piques an interest. "Queenie requested me." Velvet flips her hive eyes, and meets Kari's hollow stare. "Tell me what happened to you." A sternness in her voice quickly reminds Velvet, she is not in her own home. Her head swivels around the empty halls, ensuring they are alone.

Kari's eyes swell into those vast honeycombs. "I was attacked. Mother will see you."

The flatness in her tone is unsettling. Velvet knows Kari's mind is eroding, and she had thought this would be to her advantage, but now an idea worms its way through her mind, and she can't help but wonder what sort of control Queenie may have over Kari that Velvet herself does not yet comprehend.

Despite knowing that her own strength and capabilities are growing, Velvet doesn't feel any closer to understanding the secrets that their mother is keeping from her. Though, she has already confirmed many suspicions.

"Thank you, Kari." Her sister steps aside and opens the door leading down to a concrete cellar.

Just before she begins her descent, Velvet needs one last thing for her own peace of mind.

"Kari." Her sister's pulsing hive eyes meet her own. "Jump up and down."

Before she's even finished speaking, Kari begins squatting and jumping to the point that the crown of her head brushes against the ceilings high above with each vault.

"That's good. Go back to whatever Queenie told you to do." The revelation sends a jolt of excitement through her that carries Velvet down the stairs as if she were gliding on air.

"Good evening mother, how are you?" Despite being below ground, Velvet notices how warm it is amidst the cinderblock walls. Then she notices the latest editions to her mother's sanctuary — a myriad of space heaters.

Queenie stirs from her nightly meal, the viscera of which drips down her chin onto the thin mattress, which she sits atop. "Oh, my sweet Mel." She says warmly, swallowing the remnants of her dinner between words. "Please, sit. Update me."

"Everything has been moved and everyone has been divided per your instructions. We have drones rotating between each location, along with a handful of specialized workers. The brood is contained two houses down the street, overseen by a sister I have personally selected. Dezi, if you recall?" She hopes her mother's memory isn't as sharp as she fears it to be. This might be a make-or-break point, but she needs Dezi in charge. If only for a little longer.

"Dezi." Queenie wipes at the dark maroon pooling on the cleft of her chin. "It rings a bell. I have born so many daughters — and now sons — that I hardly remember every single name. Though, I pride myself on how many I do know. When did she assimilate?" Her mother's stare is curious, yet there's a threat there. An invitation for Velvet to slip up.

"I do not remember exactly, but she is quite intelligent, and I believe serves you loyally. Not to mention her youthful strength."

"Sounds like you my sweet." Queenie pauses to snack on something small and pungent. "Well, good then. Bring her by tomorrow. So that I might jog my memory."

"Of course Mother," Mel says bowing her head enough to

hide her eyes and the ill intentions she has behind them. "I might add that your nomadic workers will have a home base in the two buildings diagonal from here, overseen by me of course."

"Perfect, my sweet, and where is Sierra? Neither she nor her parents have been seen lately, and a mother worries."

Velvet has rehearsed for this question. "Please, do not be angry mother, but I do not know. All three disappeared shortly after the move. No one has seen any of them. I fear her mind suffered too much at the hands of . . ." She trails off, careful not to misspeak. "At the hands of her captor. I think he may have lacked the restraint needed for the operation. Either way, it seemed that she hadn't been the same since that first night."

Velvet can feel her jaw grinding forcefully. It's something she cannot hide, but she will hope her mother sees it as a worrisome tic and not indicative of the lies Velvet currently spews.

"Interesting. Maybe I said something that *made* her leave?" Queenie taps at her chin and laughs at the crimson that comes away on the tip of her finger. "Her mind always seemed — *easy to split.*"

"Agreed." Now is the perfect chance for Velvet to investigate Kari. Successfully changing the subject she asks, "Speaking of, I noticed Kari behaving rather . . . *strangely*. Might you have any idea why, mother?"

Queenie looks her up and down, yet Velvet stands strong. Unfortunately, she is no less worried about the repercussions that her mother might have in store.

"She can't tell me how she came across the information," her golden hive eyes bore into Velvet. "But she went out on her own in search of a very intriguing man who she felt would strengthen our family. Only to be *attacked*." A sudden change in her tone and the creases in Queenie's face highlight the venom behind her voice.

"Attacked?" That bit the old man had failed to relay to Velvet, yet it was the exact same word that Kari had used only moments prior

"Yes! My most precious firstborn! I believe someone may be aware of our presence."

Velvet fears this is where her mother will regret bringing them out of the cave.

"And when I find out who did this to my precious daughter, I will feast on every last bit of their entrails, ensuring that they are alive long enough to watch me do it!" Her voice drips with fury, and Velvet intelligently closes herself off from her own emotions. Sensations that are always more powerful when in her mother's presence. Otherwise, the signs of terror would likely overwhelm and betray her.

"U-understood mother." A flicker of surprise catches Velvet off guard at hearing the hitch in her voice. "What do you need from the workers and I in the morning?" This is the real reason Queenie would want her to be here each night. To obtain the next day's orders for the workers.

"I need you to hunt." Queenie stands tall, shedding her wrappings of blankets, and revealing a form that seems alien even to Velvet. Her mother appears taller, bonier, and yet, her muscles appear more taught and toned than ever. "I need to feast on a very specific meal my sweet."

"Of course, mother, anything." A brief rattle weasels out of Velvet and the fear she feels looking at her mother seems foreign. Everything before now, she knows was worry, but this emotion is abject fear. An emotion she'd forgotten about the moment she transcended the realm of humanity.

"My sweet *likkle* scarlet one." Their eyes lock on one another, and Velvet doesn't have to hear what her mother needs. She can see it in her mind's eye as if her thoughts have been invaded. The thoughts should shake her to her core, but this new information does nothing for her. Not when there is an overwhelming dread from the invasive images overrunning her mind.

With that eating at her, there is an urge to remove herself from this den, so Velvet nods her affirmation, and Queenie bids her adieu with a thick sweetened kiss.

The next thing Velvet knows, she is back within the walls of her own sanctuary, and the nectar still lingers its last dregs on her lips. All that's left for her to do this evening is decide where she will hunt for the children that her mother so desperately craves.

21
REUNITED

Ghini has one word on her mind as she and Bernie watch Legends leave the precinct.

Fucker.

The plan had been to wait for Legends to leave before confronting Dak. Ghini has never enjoyed the guy's obtuse personality.

Only now, she might be incapable of ignoring the urge to get in his face and hurl a few too many choice words regarding how the man had murdered her friend. A gentle soul she still can't believe was responsible for the kidnappings.

However, the closer the young detective gets, the more she notes how he looks unusually subdued this evening. She knows the guy had been injured during the skirmish with Todd, but she thinks how he must have had a long day to have such an abnormally flat demeanor.

A female detective meets him at the building's front entrance and the pair climb into her car before they roll out of the parking lot without so much as a second thought.

The twilight hour is upon them, but they've been waiting patiently for over a day.

Ghini no longer knows where Dak lives and without a cell phone, *her* cellphone, pre-programmed with an assortment of numbers, she couldn't contact him either. So, finding out that Dak was not at work the day prior had been a difficult blow. This meant they had to return to Samuel's, where she and Bernie spent the next twenty-four hours on edge, sleeping in shifts.

Tonight, they've already watched Dak go in, Legends has clocked out, and the only thing left to do is wait for Dak to have his first cigarette. It only takes another fifteen minutes before the detective's dreads can be spotted swaying back and forth along his back while he makes his way across the street to *their* park bench.

"Alright, let's go."

"So, that's the guy?"

"Yeah, that's him," Ghini says pulling the keys from the 250's ignition and sliding out of the cab.

"Funny. Older than I imagined. That how you like 'em?"

Ghini doesn't offer Bernie anything more than a quick glare as if to say, *there's no time for that.* After spending the last day with Bernie, she's noticed that he is nothing like his uncle.

At first, if she had a single word to describe the boy, it would have been *stoic*, a tiny replica of Samuel. But in actuality, he was only quiet until he started talking. Then it was hard to shut him up. Something that brought their first encounter into perspective. But she likes that about Bernie. He's his own person, and Ghini cannot help but enjoy the boy's company despite her overwhelming anxiety.

"Dakota," Ghini calls out with restraint in her voice as they reach the other side of the street.

Dak looks up with the flame of his lighter flickering

against his dark eyes. It takes him a second to register the pair walking toward him, but when he does, he bursts upward from the bench and runs to embrace Ghini in a grizzled hug.

Clutched to his barreled chest, she gets a strong whiff of him and is disappointed that he no longer smells like she remembers. The cologne, the body wash, it's all changed. His entire musk is different. It's more artificial than floral and earthy like she remembers.

"Where have you been?" He shouts like a panicked mother as he presses her away from his embrace. "I thought you were dead!"

That tickles a snicker out of her. "Nope. Though did come close at least once or twice."

He looks at her with a tilted peculiarity in his eyes. The worry and confusion ebb from his voice, "What's that supposed to mean?" He notices Bernie standing behind her. "And who's the young gun?"

"It's a long story, but this is Samuel's nephew." She waves the boy forward, "Bernie, Dak. Dak, Bernie." She says gesturing for the two to shake hands or hug or whatever it is that men do when they meet another male for the first time.

"Didn't know Clemens had family," Dak says dryly, extending a hand toward Bernie.

"Did ya ever ask?" The boy returns the flat remark.

"No, I guess not." The two men lock eyes and share a brief yet hearty laugh. "Where is the old coot anyhow?"

Despite having rehearsed what they were going to say, it doesn't make things any easier. "We don't know," Bernie interjects, breaking the silence. "But we guess that he's been taken."

Dak doesn't miss a beat. "By the women?" He whispers, with a morbid concern etched across his tired eyes.

This was something neither Bernie nor Ghini had

prepared for, and the rushed wide-eyed glances between them communicate that swiftly to Dak.

"I think we need to compare notes," he says pulling out his phone. "While you've been missing, a lot's happened. Not even sure where to begin. As a friend though, I hope to say, I'm sorry for your loss Ghini."

She knows he is talking about Todd, and not Samuel. But still, those condolences catch her by surprise. The pang in her chest is one she doesn't want to fight, but she does need to keep it bottled up. She nods in such a way as to tell Dak to continue.

"Okay, but more than that, there have been some concerning developments, and you'll need to see and hear some things."

That's when they all gather around a nearby picnic table and Dak plays for them the two audio tracks comparing Ghini's voice to the mysterious woman's. Afterward, he pulls up the image of Detective Bradley's eyes during that fateful press conference. He explains the paths that his investigation into the missing men had taken, and then there are his pictures from the other evening. He hasn't shown them to anyone, but there they have it. Legends with the Kalisch girl. The red-haired girl, the deaths of the Kalischs, leaving Legends alive, and then there's the last photo — those sapphire-pitted eyes.

The images are terrifying and rock Ghini to her core, but she can't explain them. Sure, she knows what they are dealing with, but it will not get them any closer to understanding the *why* of it all. Nonetheless, she is impressed with Dak and all of his detective work. Hopefully, she can convince the seasoned investigator to believe what Bernie and she have come here to explain.

"We have our own evidence to share, except most of it is

anecdotal," Bernie explains before Ghini can pull out the yellow notebook she took from the Montoyas.

Dak assures them that's fine and beckons Bernie to continue, but instead, the young man says, "I don't quite feel safe out here in the open. I'm here to get my uncle back, and can't do that if we all end up monster food. I also don't like how warm it is tonight. My gut says they won't be as afraid to hunt during the night in weather like this."

Confusion etches itself across Dak's aging face, but Ghini gathers what her companion is saying, and makes the call. "Okay, let's go. Dak, come with us to Samuel's. We can go over everything there. But let's get out of here before we put ourselves in further danger. Who knows how many people are working alongside Bradley within the precinct . . ."

Although, Ghini is quite certain that she can add at least one name to that list.

The worry shows on Dak's face and he agrees, "Alright. I'll grab my keys and check out some surveillance equipment. I've got a feeling we'll need it, and no one will bat an eye. Give me fifteen?"

They agree, and Dak jogs back into the city building while Ghini and Bernie nervously hurry to Samuel's truck. Ghini hits unlock only when they're within inches of the door handle. She hops in through the passenger side and slides across the bench seat, while Bernie follows her into the cab.

They sit in silence for just over ten minutes when Dak exits the building and breaks for his old caddy with urgency. He pulls up behind them, the headlights blinding Ghini's rearview mirror as she pulls away from the building.

Only after they have entered the highway into the hills, does the silence of the truck's cab break.

"Do you think we can trust him?"

Ghini looks over to Bernie and once more she sees the

child, not the man. The concern on his face pangs her heart deeply, and she wonders if that was a look on her own daughter's face nearly a year ago.

Had someone she trusted asked her to believe them?

"Honestly? I don't know. But it's a risk I'm willing to take. You've got the fire extinguisher?"

Bernie nods. "You've got the shotgun?"

She reaches beneath the bench seat and reveals the stock, "never going to leave home without it ever again."

22

LUCK

When Velvet returned to Legends' home that following night, the scent of decay, desperate to stay, clung to the air with a weighty odor.

She had enjoyed it. Despite knowing its source.

Her original plan had been to return and burn the bodies, but the fragrant air tasted sweet on her tongue. Alone in the house, she reconsidered her plan. Like a magnet, the scent of rot settling in pulled Velvet to the odor's source.

The master bedroom.

There, the entire Kalisch family grew rigid and began their long journey of decay amidst the muggy summer heat. Velvet knows this urge is not normal, and her desperate need for an explanation has begun consuming her.

Leading to this moment.

She enters through the breezeway on the side of Queenie's home, sure to time her morning arrival around her mother welcoming the day's hatchlings. The thin wood panel-lined passage gives way to an open area kitchen and living space. Sat like a club bouncer on a stool, is old and weathered

Clemmy — as she has taken to calling her little pet. "Hey there Clemmy."

"Mornin' Ms. Velvet." He says gruffly.

She likes Clemmy. He's no-nonsense. Even now, with his personality and life stripped from him, he behaves differently than the other drones. She is quite glad the old geezer had made it to her first — before Queenie could sink her claws into him.

Inside the home's core, just past the living space, a chorus line of hatchlings halts her progress. This is new behavior. Now, a select few workers orchestrate the newborns' parade down to Queenie rather than her coming to them.

In the cave, Queenie had always gone to their dank little nursery. Now they come to her.

This is quite possibly the best-case scenario for Velvet. There will be a funnel of her sisters pouring down into the cellar, and she will have easy access to her primary target — Kari.

After navigating around the shrinking line, Velvet finds her sister. She stands statuesque, like a member of the Welsh Guard. In fact, Kari may not have moved an inch since the last time Velvet had seen her the day prior.

The remaining newborns and their shepherds hardly pay the pair any mind. As the last stragglers enter the stairwell, Velvet maneuvers herself quietly and slowly into Kari's ear.

"Good morning sister."

"Good morning Velvet." Her affect is still flat, but there does appear to be more color to her skin today. The sickly grey and green tints from the night before now faded. Allowing her skin to return to taught and luscious perfection.

Velvet flips her eyes and catches Kari's stare. She needn't do anything more than nod to the side with a beckoning finger for her sister to follow into an adjoining room. Once certain that they were not seen, Velvet quietly eases the door shut with such tenderness that it hardly offers even the most muffled of squeaks.

Alone, Velvet looks over her sister, and in the briefest of seconds, she experiences a flicker of pity for Kari. There had always been tension between them, but this pathetic figure before her must not even have the mental bandwidth to generate an iota of tension with Velvet.

Fortunately, this sort of deference is the most perfect state of being Velvet could have asked of her sister. The giddying joy worms into the depths of her being, overtaking any sympathy she must have had for the woman.

"Kari, I need you to do something for me."

She grabs her sister by the face and delivers as much nectar as she can muster. The saliva trails briefly from their lips when they part. Velvet watches as her sister's eyes waver with life, if only briefly, before that dull, glass-like stare returns.

"Okay, Kari. I need you to tell me what you've seen, but Queenie forced you to forget." Velvets words are well rehearsed, and she is certain that Kari will deliver exactly what she is looking for.

Only, Kari doesn't answer.

There's a lull in the air. The lack of reaction feels like a chasm between the two. Velvet needs confirmation, something she suspects her sister is well capable of supplying. However, quite likely, forbidden to say.

Just as Velvet is about to utter another command, Kari's voice leaks from her throat, quiet and soft, but sounding more alive than it has in some time. "Mother. Mother told me, I am not to tell Mel what I saw. *Important.* Do not tell Mel." Her speech is fragmented and shaky.

"Of course," Velvet is quick on her feet though. She will

rethink her strategy in the hope that semantics might be her saving grace. "What did she say about telling Velvet though?"

"Mel is Velvet."

Velvet tries another tactic. "What about the daughter she calls her *likkle* scarlet one?"

This pause is longer. The wheels turn inside her sister's head, slowly and without precision it would seem. "Mother calls you... But she said no Mel. Mel is Velvet. Velvet is . . ."

The strain of processing the request through her mental fog appears to have an almost livening effect on Kari. She becomes more animated. Her brow furrows, and the thoughts behind almost seem to induce physical pain. Velvet half expects her sister to have an aneurysm or a stroke on the spot.

Not that she even thinks their kind are capable of being burdened with such afflictions.

A large gasp echoes from Kari's gaping mouth and her eyes grow wide. The words that follow come to life with the passion of the sister that Velvet remembers, and though she is not glad to see this version of Kari, Velvet is optimistic that she can get exactly what she desires from her.

"Tell the *likkle scarlet one*. What has Mother forced you to forget? Remember it for me."

She feels the weight of her sapphire stare pulsing down onto her sister with intense gravity. A spark of joy continues slithering its way through Velvet as Kari's eyes swell. She knows the words are about to flow from her.

"Mother eats the dead." She says with a rattle of something in her voice.

Fright.

"What do you mean?" They all eat the dead. They all did that before they were even assimilated. This isn't news.

"Mother eats sisters and brothers." Her body language stays animated, yet hypnotic. Her tone hasn't wavered from that horror-stricken rattle. The look on her face is what Velvet would expect to see of someone hearing all this for the first time.

"Go on."

"Queenie eats the bodies. Some die in hatching. Some she kills in anger. Some she kills for pleasure. All of them, she eats." Each word comes out as if it were a brand new revelation to the woman standing before her.

"Why does she eat them?" This is the reason she has come here.

Velvet isn't exactly shocked or appalled by the behavior, it's not like any of them are human anyway. There has to be something deeper. A route cause, a *need*, why would she need to eat *their* dead?

"I do not know."

"Damnit." She swears quietly.

Of course, her cravings the night prior make more sense, but there's an innate understanding of the desire as well. So it could hardly be labeled a revelation.

What she needs to know is, what happens after? Why does Queenie need to do this covertly? Why sacrifice her firstborn's mind for such an inconsequential secret?

After Velvet dismisses Kari, telling her to forget this conversation, she runs down to speak with Queenie, who is behaving strangely. More precocious and child-like. Velvet relays that they were not able to get her what she desired, but that they would try again the next day.

To her surprise, this version of her mother doesn't seem worried. Not even upset. She tells Velvet that it isn't important just yet, but there is something quite specific she desires from the child that Velvet brings her. They should be in shorts and a t-shirt during the first cold spell.

This feels like an oddly specific puzzle piece, and now she

just needs to understand how it fits into the grander scheme of things. She'll have plenty of time to unravel the mystery of that specific request as there are still a handful of months to come before any cold snap.

She had feared retribution for this failure, and also for *"forgetting"* to bring Dezi along with her. But Velvet hedged her bets against her own value, and that seems to have paid off. She has somehow managed to buy more time than she had expected. Why her mother so drastically changed her mind, Velvet cannot be sure. Nonetheless, she refuses to look this gift horse in the mouth.

With that, Queenie nonchalantly dismisses Velvet with a wave of the hand, and she is quick to take her leave. Atop the stairs, she runs into Clemmy once more, and something dawns on her. "Clemmy, where will I find your little friend, Ghini Freeman?"

"Likely, at my place."

"And where is that?"

"Up the road."

An idea sparks within Velvet, bringing a devilish smirk to her typically dour expression. Though, for it to work, she'll first need to quickly circle back and pay Kari one final visit.

23

THE NOTEBOOK

October 30th, 2011
8:04 am

Momma's been down there almost a decade now. I haven't noted anything since the escape yesterday, and I shot her. Buckshot to the back of her legs, but she kept trying to run. The wound didn't seem to do a single damn thing to slow her down. She limped, but there wasn't any pain on her face as she pushed through it.

Momma may have been let out. Can't say for sure. She fed though. It was too late to identify the body when I found her.

After being shot she let loose the most sinister cry I've ever heard. It wasn't human.

Then came the noxious smell. Possibly a pheromone.
Something to warn others like her.
Or worse. A call for help.

Not sure if there's anything we can do to
help her.

The elders no longer want any part of her "treat-
ment" — if it can even be called that. Whether
pharmaceutical or natural, there doesn't appear to
be any remedy for her "condition." Thankfully,
they passed along many stories until now. I have
written these legends throughout several notebooks.
Some are more helpful than others.

She hardly looks like the same woman anymore.
Her features are skin and bone like a drug
addict. But she's strong. Inhumanly strong.

    October 31st, 2011
    9:15 am

Momma's legs are healed. No scars, bullet holes,
or anything. She's pacing without issue

    11:52 am

Momma's sent Lawson out for her meal.

11:59 am

Need to conduct more tests to see how to stop her. If there are more of her kind, we have to be able to stop them.

Direct Fan Test (DFT) - she curled into the blankets but moved around in the huddled mass when offered food.

12:05 pm

Flame Test (FT) - she never shies away, but the smell of burnt skin and hair is palatable in the air. High pain tolerance?

Would fit with her behavior yesterday while running with bullet holes in her legs.

That noxious smell is back.

November 4th, 2011
4:02 am

Momma woke early today. I couldn't sleep, going to check on her.

4:19 am

Sleeping Gas (SG) - Works relatively quickly, but had to pump in three times the dose that is suggested for someone of my size, and she's half that at most.

November 5th, 2011
11:10 am
Lawson left for food for Momma. I'm fearful of what, no who, he'll bring back.

11:22 am

Liquid Nitrogen Test (LNT) - I was able to disperse it with an aerosol device. She shrieked like a banshee when it touched her skin and became incredibly violent, thrashing about her cell and throwing whatever she could at me.
Noxious smell returns.
Pain tolerance less effective in cold environment?

10:45 pm

LNT 2 - I was able to use the SG on momma again. No change to dosage.
Froze left pinky toe while she slept.
She grew fitful but did not wake.
Then I smashed it with a hammer. It shattered like glass.

She began to stir, but the sleeping gas kept her under long enough.
NO noxious smell

November 7th, 2011
7:13 am

The toe is back. No scar. No sign of the previous injury. I didn't check yesterday. Looks like we can add regeneration to her abilities, on top of super reflexes, strength, and hypnosis eyes.

November 8th, 2011
6:12 am

Would a bullet to the head even work?

Or would she heal from that too?

B ernie, Ghini, and Dak have been held up in Samuel's home for several days now.

Dak has been burning through a career's worth of vacation days it feels like. But it has not been for nothing. The trio's time has been wisely spent comparing notes from the Montoya notebook and Dak's own investigations.

Surprisingly, Dak has bought into everything Bernie and Ghini have said, and he has been obsessed with the notebook since he cracked it open. Some of it reminds him of tall tales that his grandmother used to tell him and all his cousins growing up. Dak has spent the entirety of his life thinking of those as nothing more than ghost stories to tell around the campfire. But now. Now, he's not so sure. Considering the Montoya brothers were from an indigenous upbringing, it only convinces Dak further that they need to go visit granny on the reservation.

He owes her at least that much.

Dak sets down the notebook and rubs at his eyes beneath the cheaters caught at the edge of his wide nose.

"Anything substantial?" Bernie's voice is easily distinguishable as it cracks while Dak continues to massage his aching eyes.

"Well, we've got one more ability to add to the list. *Regeneration*. And by Montoya's notes here, it takes just 24 hours give or take. Seems to depend on the seriousness of the injury."

Stoicism rests across Bernie's face. As if his mind is forcing even his features to whisper. "So, how do we kill them if they can heal themselves?"

"According to these records," Dak pats the notebook as if it were a good dog. "We can burn them, and we know from Ghini's encounter with the Montoyas, that fire and explosions should work. But—" The word lingers in the air.

"We never got proof of death." Ghini strolls into the room setting down three iced coffees on the mahogany coffee table centered between them. They have all refused to give themselves any sort of break, making for long days. Outside, the sun is starting to shower through the windows with a watermelon-pink glow.

"Correct. I'm not even sure we can say that either brother

is dead. Not with so much doubt in the air." Dak chews on the edge of a pen.

Day after day it feels like they have more questions than answers. They know what can slow down these creatures, but taking them out altogether feels like a dangerous mystery left unsolved. The same question that Manny had pondered sits nestled in the center of Dak's mind.

Would a bullet to the head even work?

"We also know cold's effective," Bernie adds.

"True. That woman at the WH was without a doubt frantic to get away from the fire extinguisher and sprinklers." Ghini picks at the sleep in the corner of her eyes, which have grown dull and baggy with the lack of rest. "She'd even stripped out of her wet clothes and laid on a rock like a lizard. She needed to warm herself as quickly as possible. But she ran off without so much as her underwear. Into the forest, no less. Clearly, she has no shame."

Dak snickers at that.

"Monsters never do." Bernie's words cut the brief levity.

Dak gets up from the dinette table that has been his primary residence for several hours now and goes over to the large duffel bag they've packed. It's currently full of pistols and shotguns from Samuel's stockroom. There are also two small-sized fire extinguishers tucked into the edge pockets. The bag has some heft to it, but nothing Dak can't manage. He sets the notebook on top and plops down on the couch next to Ghini, where he picks up one of the coffees.

"So I've got an idea." He leans forward with his elbows resting on his knees. His eyes are drawn toward the fireplace across the room. His hands hold his rounded jawline, keeping him level as he gives one last consideration to the idea he is about to suggest. "We may need to go visit my granny. She told stories — ghost stories mostly — to all of us cousins around the campfire growing up. But something about this all feels familiar. Like one of her stories."

He lets gravity pull him back into the plush leather backing, his eyes traverse the stone-inlaid walls to the vaulted ceiling above, and the warm pink glow pours through several skylights overhead.

"She lives on a reservation too, and maybe there's something to the orating nature of indigenous people that allows the story to live on. I just think we need more intel."

"Agreed. But," Bernie pauses and nibbles at the end of a finger before spitting a piece of nail to the floor. "We need to be quick. I have a bad feeling that the more time we spend not stopping these things, the worse the situation will become. There're fourteen or fifteen towns in and around The Black Hills alone."

Bernie needn't say more. Dak and Ghini both understand the implications of what this could mean for the monstrous army's numbers.

That's when a large *THUMP* from somewhere outside reverberates throughout the entirety of the home. Dak notices Bernie startle, and though Ghini remains frozen like a statue, he watches her as her eyes widen.

In an instant, the lights go out. The only light left is a deepening red from the setting sun blanketing across the skylights overhead. The crimson glow seems to put them all on edge.

"Breaker must have tripped," Bernie says. "I'll go check on it. It's out in the garage."

"Kid." Bernie stutters to a halt but does not turn around as Dak gets up to put a hand on the boy's shoulder, hopefully preventing him from going off alone. "Kid. Seriously. Take a gun with you."

Bernie looks back with wide eyes and that's when Dak notices it too. A drip of sweat traces down his cheekbone.

The air's off in the house.

The summer heat is waning with the season, but the nights still tend to hold the heat and humidity more than any of them wish to tolerate.

Dak moves quickly to the duffel bag and grabs a shotgun before tucking a pistol into his waistband. Bernie follows suit.

Ghini already has a fire extinguisher nearby, and a small .22 at her side. Dak knows she hopes she won't need to use it. But the way Ghini is white-knuckling the extinguisher, tells him she is well prepared to do so.

There's another *THUMP*.

Then another.

And another.

The thumps continue until they pinpoint the silhouettes blotting out the crimson glow of the setting sun above.

Before any of them have time to register what's happening, a crash from above their heads rains glass down like a malignant hail storm.

24

PHEROMONES

As she plummets through the open air, into the home, and to the floor beneath her, a lucid moment finds Kari.

They're becoming few and far between these days.

Her boots land with a crunch atop several shards of glass. Her two sisters crash down in quick succession on either side of her.

With her eyes flipped, the darkness is difficult at first but quickly becomes easier to navigate as her eyes adjust. There are just the three humans. Kari cannot help thinking that Queenie was right. This is about to be a one-sided victory for Kari and her sisters. She will be able to return to Velvet with such pride.

No. To Queenie.

Yes. To Queenie.

That's who she is to deliver the prisoners to.

She eyes the three humans. They're ducking for cover, but she can still count each of them. One hardly appears more than a boy, and the other is a heavy-set man. Neither is her target. The third person must be.

She doesn't get a good look at the dark buzz cut diving behind a kitchen island, but there is a familiarity about her presence. This must be the one that her mother tasked her with.

No. Not Mother.

That Velvet tasked her.

Velvet is Mother.

No.

Her mind swims in thick and sluggish thoughts. Her consciousness struggles amongst the myriad of ideas that seem both foreign and innate all at once. It makes Kari feel more like a vessel for another being than she does her own autonomous entity.

"That's her!" The woman with buzzed hair cries, finger outstretched from behind the food-laden kitchen island.

A wave of anger and hatred scorches a path through Kari. Her finger points itself back at the woman whom she recognizes but still cannot place.

Where her wound had once been, an ache boils into an intense spike of pain, before quickly subsiding into a steady stream of lava-like rage. The precursor to an eruption.

Before she can do anything, she is blindsided by the boy. He charges her, blasting a quick succession of shots from a double-barreled shotgun.

One grazes Kari, but she moves too quickly to make for an easy target. She finds cover behind a large leather couch and sees that her two sisters have also found safety behind a lazy boy and a toppled dinette table.

"For Queenie!" One of her sisters cries from behind her.

An image of their mother flashes through Kari's mind.

That first morning. She'd been wrapped up in a comforter.

Queenie had skipped and played like a child. Her hair bouncing atop the crown of her head like a black cloud, and that love, that inspiration generates the catalyst needed for Kari to act.

A scream shatters her reverie and, instinct swivels her head in the appropriate direction.

Then come the *BANGs*! Several in rapid succession.

She tucks herself tightly behind her hiding spot. A hefty *thump* is followed swiftly by an unearthly scream. The sound roars into the night air, infiltrating the darkness through the empty glass panes above.

Two more *BANGs* ring out across the room and an unholy silence consumes the dark living space. There's a scent in the air. Her brain fires images of pain and death. Not so much images, but memories. Ones where she has experienced tragedy. The death of her parents. Putting her dog down. It's those ghostly echoes of emotions that run through her.

The anger spikes.

Kari has lost a sister.

The sweet scent begins to sour. It grows foul and fills her with white-hot rage. Fuel to her erupting need for vengeance. Instinct takes control of her legs, and she leaps over the couch like a free runner. Her feet collide with the floor, and she rolls toward where the percussive *BANGs* had come from.

"We gotta go!" A sharp male voice screams from behind Kari. The sound is different and she realizes it's echoing off the linoleum tile in the kitchen. She looks up and the area is bathed in a cold white glow from the broken skylights above.

Shots fire.

Kari ducks behind an old wooden chest situated as a coffee table. "I think that smell's," the man's voice gags, "I think it's a cry for help. Like some bees or something!"

The words don't register with Kari. She sees her other

sister crouched behind the sofa. Her hive eyes are the color of almonds. But there is an intensity set in them. They tremor and Kari understands the fury her sister has. It's the same one incinerating a path throughout Kari herself.

Now's the moment for her to take charge. Kari's eyes dart away and back toward her sister. She knows with nothing more than her hives, she can silently communicate for the girl to flank around the shooter. Kari is going to take the large man down, and her sister can go for the boy.

In sync, they tumble over their respective hideouts and zig their way through the furniture. Kari looks up and sees a man with long dreadlocks slithering like snakes down the sides of his head, and a skinny woman who looks familiar . . .

Something clicks inside her head and it slows her movements.

This is the woman. Who shot me.

Her fury at the realization breaks her unbridled rush just enough for her pace to falter and feel something small and viciously fast break through her arm. The force sends her into a tight tailspin down to the ground.

She's been shot.

But it doesn't hurt. The rage inside her is so much more commanding. She gives into that rage. This woman and her friend have now both shot Kari.

They both must pay.

"You will pay!" The voice that emanates from her throat is not her own. It's hoarse with rage, and the words scorch the back of her throat with venomous ferocity.

"That's the one! From the other day! The one that got Samuel!" The woman's voice screams.

You will pay. You will pay. You will pay. The threat choruses through Kari's mind.

Kari's movements become jungle-cat-like. She crouches

and quietly navigates the space. She can hear her prey breathing, their hearts pumping rapidly with excess adrenaline. The footsteps on the tiled floor can be heard slowly backing away. Meanwhile, her remaining sister inches around, back somewhere behind her, stealthily moving toward the kitchen.

Blinded by hatred, Kari emerges from her hiding space without thinking twice. She lands crouched on her feet, ready to dive, when she is hit, hard. The thought of her arm having been hit twice inflames her emotions further, but the force doesn't stop. The momentum spreads out across a larger swathe of her body. Once more she feels herself falling. Only this time a weight atop her is making the free fall alongside her and causes her body to impact the ground twice with the smallest of bounces.

Tilting her head down, Kari realizes the boy has wrapped her up like a football tackle. He seems so puny in comparison to the man. Regardless, Kari knows that there isn't a human alive that she can't handle. A fist crashes into the side of her face, and though it does nothing more than turn her head, the thought of being touched infuriates her. Something maniacal blows from her chest, once more scorching her throat.

Another fist crashes into her. Then another. But the chortling doesn't cease. Kari can't feel a thing. A fly would be more of a nuisance. She flips her eyes and looks up at the boy straddling her.

He has piercingly cold eyes. For a brief second, lucidity returns to Kari. The rage is washed away in the cold sea of that utterly human sense known as terror.

She snaps back to her fury in just enough time to snag the boy's wrist, preventing the butcher's knife in his hand from slicing at her abdomen. She bucks the boy off and spins into a sprinter's starting position.

The boy looks familiar in the way that some strangers do.

She can't put her finger on it, but the thought is gone before it could ever take root. Her feet have a mind of their own. With intense force, she leaps at him and lowers her bony shoulder into his sternum. The violent check sends him flying the few feet between him and the wall.

Images flash through her mind.

Velvet.

She remembers throwing the little bitch.

But no. It's not the red hair.

Then comes a fleeting reverie. It's not bright red hair soaring through the air, and Kari isn't responsible. Queenie is. And the woman has long dark hair.

A scream snaps her from the waking dream. In the kitchen, she sees her sister crouched atop the short-haired woman. There's blood on the ground around them.

Her mind flashes more snapshots from the past.

A shock of red carpet zips back and forth as claws dive from above at a pathetic creature left lame across the ground.

Something hard smashes Kari across the face and this time it hurts. If only a bit. She reels to the ground and that's when she sees it.

The body on the cave floor. There's blood everywhere. The black cloud that made Kari think of motherly love, now stood over the bloodied body. The downed woman's leg twitched —

Another smash across Kari's face forces her to come back to reality as her head cracks the linoleum behind her. Her mind attempts to drift back to the cave.

The leg twitches on the ground.

The black cloud viciously bobs up and down.

The *BANGs* return, and another paralyzing scream claws Kari's mind out beneath another memory. Four or five more *BANGs* boom out in quick succession, and things grow eerily silent.

In the cave the silence was palpable. Her mother sees her, and the deep crimson streams that flood Queenie's chin unsettles Kari most. But there was the woman on the ground. A sister. A sister. Her name was — Kari can't recall. But she had angered Mother. The look behind her mother's honey-gold eyes told Kari all she needed to know. Kari wasn't supposed to be here.

Again, a collision jars the side of Kari's face. She looks up and finds the boy holding a large red tube. There's blood all across the bottom end, which he used to strike Kari. She feels the anger welling up behind her breast.

The fog that rolls in when she no longer feels in control, is now materializing around her.

A loud *whoosh* brings with it, a white blanket of cold all across her body. She feels herself freezing. That fog in her mind grows denser, thick like soup, and the resulting effect on her vision is debilitating. She feels drunk. Her head is spinning. She can't orient. A violent sense of illness burrows into her gut.

Footsteps fade away from her and then rapidly return.

"Where's my uncle?" The wobbling figure ahead of her asks in his tattered voice.

She looks away from the man and sees her other sister lifeless on the ground. Her eyes are as human as that of the boy currently standing over her. His figure becomes more clear with each passing second. Still, her stomach roils. Her head feels light. The metallic object he's holding crashes across her face and this hurts. Like the first bit of pain from a toothache. Still, it is the first time she has felt such a sensation in months.

She does not care for it.

Kari snarls at the boy standing over her. "I probably fed him to Mother or ate him myself!"

The boy screams and something punches her multiple

times in the gut. There's a swift force behind it. Otherwise, she hardly thinks she would have registered the object, but then her ears stop ringing. She looks down and sees the deep violet stains pooling out of her abdomen.

Above her, the boy's face is twisted in such disgusting fury that she's reminded of her loathsome grandmother. Her horrid boyfriend, Jason. And — then she sees it.

That red shock of carpet. Velvet. In the depths of her mind, those words from her sister co-mingle with the boy's. Combining past and present into one seamless moment.

"Listen here you bitch."

You will do exactly as I say.

"Otherwise, I'm going to blow your fucking brains out! You hear me?"

Good. Now take two of your sisters up the road to this address. It isn't far. Everyone there dies, except this woman. Bring her to me.

"I swear if you don't tell me where he is!"

I will kill you. Poor, pathetic, Kari.

Those cold sapphire eyes come back to her, and she looks up expecting to see the bright red fuzz, but the only person there is the boy and his gun.

"You should never have come here."

I wasn't supposed to be here.

She sees her mother eating the woman, except, she isn't a woman, she's too small.

QUEENIE WAS WRAPPED in several loose-fitting layers, but she braved the night to feel the warm air while taking in the light from the nearly full moon. It was a gloriously bright evening. It would soon be at its fullest, and she wondered how bright that would be. The entirety of the hills all around her are swathed in its luminescence.

Then she heard the first scream, if ever so faintly. Instincts inform her as to what was transpiring. But she waited. The smell of death wafted in the air and grew shortly after a second more abrupt scream. There had been several loud *BANGs* as well.

The gunfire did not alarm her. Instead, she curiously sat back and thought about the weakness of some of her children. She would not even bother to reclaim their bodies for herself. Then came the third scream echoing ever so briefly.

As Death's odor wafts down to her on the night breeze, Queenie takes note that the scent does nothing to elicit anything from her. Even the knowledge that the final cries had been from her firstborn. She couldn't help but think about how the meek will not inherit the Earth. She and all of her daughters will.

Tires suddenly screech up the road and go blaring past the front of her home only seconds later. Queenie knows that despite winning the battle this evening, whoever it was that had culled her weaker children, correctly felt they should fear retribution, as the war was far from over.

ACKNOWLEDGMENTS

Thank you to everyone in the Kindle Vella community where *Season of The Monster* was exclusively serialized.

There were so many fantastic individuals who helped me grow as a writer, a marketer, and even as a reader. This is a passionate and devoted community of writers, to which, I am wholeheartedly grateful.

Specifically, I want to throw thanks to the Hella Vella team of Azrielle Lawless & Airik Eisen. Thank you for having me on your shows for interviews and talking with me about all my stories.

Tess Combs, you literally financed my first-ever ad campaign. No, it wasn't much, but you saw something that made you believe in me and SOTM. For that, I am indebted to you.

Zack Lester, man you rock, and you know it. I'm glad I've got a guy in this world that I can turn to about all this writing stuff. It also helps that we can always talk about basketball, and not to mention that you're as mad a hatter as I!

Tirzah Hawkins, I could devote pages to you here. Your advice, your support, your inspirational success, the works you've put out there to help educate new authors like me, your lack of gatekeeping — I mean seriously, I could go on forever. You're an amazing human, and I value you so much.

Of course, I don't know where I would be without my Story Stash peeps like Jen Sequel, Des Sweets, Coda Languez, C.L. Slias, Kell Frillman, Kim Riehle, Liz Johnson, LJ Vitanza, Tasha Creed, S RC Johnson, and those other members I've already mentioned. You all are extended family at this point!

A special shout-out to Esmée L., despite being a world away, it seems like you've always been there to help me out as I've started my journey. Thank you, and best of luck on your literary journey, I can't wait to see what comes of it!

Thanks go out to my friends Roland G. (VVolfgxng on Spotify & Apple Music) and Mitchell Hynds (YouTube). You guys are not only chasing your dreams but have been there for me on my journey. I cannot wait to see what you both accomplish!

To my Mizzou Tigers Family, Dennis (and Angelica), Armani, Logan, Kevin N., Erin O., Josh Z., Tyger L., Noah T., and so many more, thank you for your love and support. Especially, during the dark times.

Lastly, thank you to my family. We haven't always gotten along, but even when I've behaved a bit like a monster myself, you all have been there for me. Thank you, Mom, Dad, and Grant. I love you, guys.

CHILL

Queenie wakes amidst a nest of drones. Their body heat radiates through the hoard of thick comforters that she nestles herself into each night. The warmth is comforting, and the addition of several space heaters makes stirring from her cozy slumber all the easier.

The house feels especially toasty this morning. The way a ski lodge might provide a quiet cozy ambiance despite the thick blanket of white frost outside its large gleaming windows.

She can hear the HVAC humming with an added intensity as if it's been working overtime throughout the night. A strange thought considering how hot and muggy it has been over the course of the past week.

She doesn't often leave the basement but wants to see outside this morning.

She had a dream last night.

This is a rarity for Queenie. However, when her unconscious being does manage to distract her mind, she knows the images playing out before her are not of her own design.

They are from assimilating. There had been the long sleep. The one where muddied visions ran like a spotty film reel, generating mosaics from the echoes beyond a cramped cocoon.

Experiences lived, but not by her own conscious, always come to her as if she were only a patron at the show, and not the actor.

This dream had been different, though.

For the first time in the space of her existence, she had been the actor. From her chrysalis, she listened as *her* founder, *her* mother spoke with someone about a phoenix, and avoiding the long sleep. They had made plans. Queenie had listened. But were those plans ever explicitly shared with Queenie herself?

Reliving the dream, her mind sinks around her. Swallowing her consciousness into the dark void of her mind. There's a memory that plays out before her like a movie in this dark abyss.

Walter.

The name comes to her without more than a flash of his face. Despite this playing out inside her own mind, Queenie doesn't feel like this is her reverie. Instinctively, she knows it must belong to someone else.

The wise drone had taught her many things in the short time they shared. More souvenirs of her life are lodged in her long dream-like memories, but they always remain jumbled. Queenie cannot be sure what to make of this newest reverie from her most recent metamorphosis months. Irrespective, she is certain this is a problem. One she must solve before the air cools and her daughters begin to dwindle.

Those incapable of adapting, at least.

Atop the cellar stairs, she turns for the front sitting room. Her attention is drawn out of the large bay window that overlooks the sprawling backyard, before dropping off into the valley below. From her high vantage in the hills, she can watch as puffs of steam slink skyward from the thin sprawling cowboy town.

There isn't a single pockmark of a cloud blemishing the entire horizon. Yet, there is a coldness about it. As if a layer of ice has subdued the cerulean sky overhead, making it a blanched version of its former self.

Opposite the window is the thermostat. Its 'smart' display reads that the temperature indoors is 85, but outside, the temp is less than half that — 41 degrees.

The thought of such cold elicits a primitive anxiety within her breast. She pivots her attention back to the view below. The quiet bustle of life has yet to cease in the hilly valley town.

From this Godly vantage, Queenie finally feels worthy of this namesake of hers. A feeling that doesn't always present itself, year in and year out.

Her omnipotence looms over the kingdom. The silent haven her children can thrive in, subject to Queenie's rule, of course.

Except for the one.

So many of her children have done exactly as she required of them. They have grown her family, rescuing multitudes of young and innocent women from the lives they have been persecuted to live. But more than that, they have subjugated so many indolent men. To this, Queenie sees her own benevolent grace. She has given them purpose in her new order. Entire families have become her offspring, and this thrills her to no end.

As her family has grown, so too has her body; and in rather unexpected ways. The endless supply of sustenance that her daughters procure for her has led to some startling physical changes that Queenie has never known before. It's now at the point that she may have to begin worrying about ducking through the occasional doorway. A catch-twenty-two of her daughters' devoutness toward catering all her needs.

The sun's rays peer through the window and caress her ebony cheeks in a gentle warmth. A strength seems to well up inside her as if the rays were concentrated caffeine fueling her energy for the day. Beneath her added layers, she can feel her muscles flex with a surging strength fortified through the warm glow.

The surge in energy amplifies her already waxing hunger, which is becoming more ravenous with every passing day. Her body is well aware and well-trained to consume an abundance at this time each year in preparation for her next long sleep. Only now, the insatiable hunger returns soon after each meal with a searing pang unlike any she has known before.

But she has a solution for this. She cannot afford to waste precious entrées on her children. Yet, she had felt ingenious when devising a way to obtain an endless supply of food for her children. This meant the most delectable courses would be reserved for Queenie alone.

Abandoning the window, in favor of navigating her way through the home and into the garage, she stalls. Inside the two-car concrete cube, her breath leaves her lungs in a ghastly vapor. This ignites a fiery anger within Queenie.

The cool air pierces through the lingering warmth that the motherly sun had embraced her with. Needles poke through her, draining the warmth and pleasure she had just known. The discomfort spreads like a plague to her limbs. She is well aware of her slowing gait. The stiffness in her joints infects her mind with a virus that seems to beleaguer her thinking.

The multitude of animals yap, bark, and squawk at her

from behind the locks of their cramped cages. There, however, is no reason to pay them any mind. Queenie's curiosity lay with their keeper, who likely would not have survived the night.

The daughter with the unfortunate task sits limply against an ancient folding chair with her head lolled forward. Queenie thinks the woman must have surely passed in the night, despite her puffy parka with its fur-lined hood. Yet, when she grabs the woman's upper arm with enough force to pierce through the woman's jacket into the warm flesh beneath, she stirs. A set of gentle hazel eyes look up at Queenie in bewilderment.

"Mother?" The woman inquires with concern. "You shouldn't be out here." The girl's pale complexion is natural, but the flush in her cheeks speaks to the surprise and worry she has upon seeing her mother in this cool and confined space.

"I can go wherever I please," Queenie is harsher with her tone than intended, but she doesn't realize it. Her thinking has become crowded by a beastly rage.

"O-o-of course. I jus—"

The woman never has a chance to finish uttering her sentiment as Queenie's hands fly to the woman's head. Her long and slender fingers claw around the woman's skull, which feels delicate and weak in Queenie's hands. Though, she does not hear the brutish howl her lungs uncage as her hands violently snap at the woman's head.

As Queenie's adrenaline settles with the gratification of a successful hunter, she stares down into a gaze permanently twisted 180 degrees in the wrong direction.

Looks like breakfast will be more filling than anticipated.

The thought brings a toothy grin to her cheeks and only

broadens with the distress the girl inside her feigns for the limp corpse Queenie begins to tow at her side.

She enters the home with the body dragging behind her, the way a child might drag their doll behind them while in search of their parents following a bad dream. She detests that her meal will be so fresh, but this is one she is certain should be enjoyed as soon as possible.

ABOUT THE AUTHOR

AJ Humphreys is an emerging author of thrillers, horrors, and mysteries. *Season of The Monster | SUMMER* is the second part of his debut novel.

When AJ isn't writing he can often be found in a hammock reading, maybe while camping, but almost always with his best buddy, Kobe The Husky at his side. Together, they both enjoy hiking and swimming, especially.

He also operates as an amateur landscape and wildlife photographer, which fits in well with his thirst for outdoor adventuring.

Subscribe to *The Authors' Journey* Newsletter at readajhvellas.com and stay in the loop on new releases, serial writings, as well as merchandise, photography, and other fun giveaways/announcements.

AJ currently lives in Urbana, IL, where he works as a server part-time to support his dream of writing full-time.

AJ loves to connect with readers and writers, so make sure to check out all of his social media platforms!

amazon.com/author/ajhumphreyswrites
facebook.com/ajhumphreyswrites
goodreads.com/ajhumphreys
instagram.com/ajhumphreyswrites
tiktok.com/@aj_humphreys
twitter.com/ajhumphreys2
youtube.com/@ajhumphreyswrites